"Wait a minute. You're a woman," the prince said, as though that thought had just presented itself to him.

Emma Valentine felt color rushing into her cheeks and she silently begged it to stop. Here she was, formless and stodgy in her chef's whites. No makeup, no stiletto heels. Hardly the picture of the femmes fatales he was undoubtedly used to.

"That's a rare ability for insight you have there, Your Highness," she snapped before she could stop herself. And then she winced. She was going to have to do better than that if she was going to keep this relationship on an even keel.

But he was ignoring her dig. Nodding, he stared at her with a speculative gleam in his golden eyes. "I've been looking for a woman, but you'll do."

Emma blanched, stiffening. "I'll do for what?"

Amusement sparkled in the prince's eyes. He was certainly enjoying this. And that only made her more determined to resist him.

"I'm the prince, remember? And we're in my castle. My orders take precedence. It's that old pesky divine rights thing...."

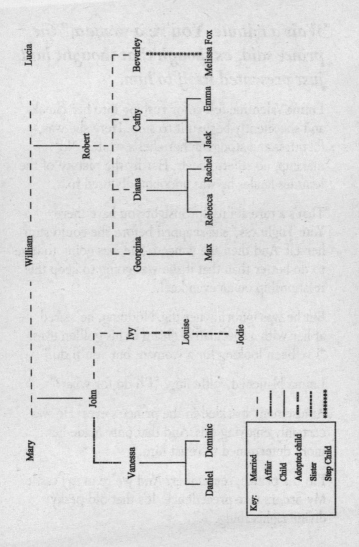

Key:
Married
Affair
Child
Adopted child
Sister
Step Child

Mary
John
Ivy
Louise
Jodie
Vanessa
Daniel
Dominic

William
Robert
Lucia
Beverley
Melissa Fox
Cathy
Jack
Emma
Diana
Rebecca
Rachel
Georgina
Max

RAYE MORGAN

The Rebel Prince

The Brides of Bella Lucia

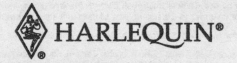

HARLEQUIN®

TORONTO • NEW YORK • LONDON
AMSTERDAM • PARIS • SYDNEY • HAMBURG
STOCKHOLM • ATHENS • TOKYO • MILAN • MADRID
PRAGUE • WARSAW • BUDAPEST • AUCKLAND

ISBN-13: 978-0-373-18258-9
ISBN-10:   0-373-18258-9

THE REBEL PRINCE

First North American Publication 2006.

Copyright © 2006 by Harlequin Books S.A.

Special thanks and acknowledgment are given to Helen Conrad
for her contribution to *The Brides of Bella Lucia* series.

This edition published by arrangement with Harlequin Books S.A.

® and TM are trademarks of the publisher. Trademarks indicated with
® are registered in the United States Patent and Trademark Office, the
Canadian Trade Marks Office and in other countries.

www.eHarlequin.com

Printed in U.S.A.

THE BRIDES OF BELLA LUCIA

A family torn apart by secrets, reunited by marriage

When William Valentine returned from the war, as a testament to his love for his beautiful Italian wife, Lucia, he opened the first Bella Lucia restaurant in London. The future looked bright, and William had, he thought, the perfect family.

Now William is nearly ninety, and not long for this world, but he has three top London restaurants with prime spots throughout Knightsbridge and the West End. He has two sons, John and Robert, and grown-up grandchildren on both sides of the Atlantic who are poised to take this small gastronomic success story into the twenty-first century.

But when William dies, and the family fight to control the destiny of the Bella Lucia business, they discover a multitude of long-buried secrets, scandals, the threat of financial ruin and, ultimately, two great loves they hadn't even dreamed of: the love of a lifelong partner, and the love of a family reunited....

**The Valentine saga continues
next month when we meet Jodie in
Wanted: Outback Wife by Ally Blake**

To Emily Ruston—
thanks for your helpful guidance
and tactful editing

CHAPTER ONE

Jet lag—maybe he could blame it on that.

Or maybe on the general state of simmering anger he'd been in since he'd been told life as he knew it was over and he was to submit meekly to living his brother's life instead. That might have thrown his aim off.

Whatever.

He'd missed the shot and he'd hit the young woman by mistake. And that was when everything began to spin out of control.

Prince Sebastian wasn't used to missing a shot— he had an arm like a rocket launcher and had once even been urged to join his country's Olympic water-polo team. He'd never injured anyone with a shot before—except other players in the generally rough play of the game he loved. But he seemed to have the reverse Midas curse these days—everything he touched went bad.

For a fraction of a heart-stopping second, he was afraid he'd killed her.

Pacio, one of the young footmen who'd been playing the game of water polo with him, said as much, swimming over to the side of the indoor castle pool behind him.

"She looks like she's dead. *Muerta*," he added for good measure.

"She's not dead," Sebastian corrected sharply, though his nerves were still jumping from that momentary fear.

Vaulting out of the pool, he kicked the still-bouncing water-polo ball out of the way and crouched over her, shaking away the water that dripped from his sleek body.

"Is she breathing?" Pacio asked with interest, climbing out of the pool as well. "Wow. She went down just like a rag doll."

Sebastian didn't bother answering. She seemed to be unconscious. Not a good sign.

"Hello," he tried, touching her shoulder. "Are you all right?"

There was no response.

He put two fingers to the pulse at her neck, glad to find it strong, then noted her chest move. She was breathing, but she looked so pale and vulnerable lying there in her cutoff jeans and sleeveless jersey top. He wanted to gather her up and get her off the cold floor. But he probably shouldn't move her. Had she hit her head on the tile? Maybe she was in shock.

Snagging a large towel someone had hung on the railing, he draped it over her and bit back frustration. Why the hell wasn't she moving? And why the hell couldn't he remember more of his decade-old life-saving classes? It was obviously time to recruit someone who knew what he was doing.

"Go get the doctor," he ordered as two others who'd been in the pool with them came up, shivering and dripping water everywhere.

"You mean Will?" Pacio asked hesitantly.

Sebastian looked up at the three young men who were staring at him blankly. "Of course I mean Will. Get him. Now."

The three of them looked surprised, but they jerked into action, hurrying off. He felt a fleeting sense of satisfaction that he'd managed to conjure up a tone of command. That was something he was going to have to do often and better if he was really going to end up as the king of Meridia—if this really wasn't just a bad dream he was going to wake up from and laugh at.

Meridia—the crazy little country that knew

him as Sebastian Edwardo Valenza Constantine Marchand-Dumontier, prince of Meridia and second son of King Donatello and Queen Marguerite, both deceased. And now that his older brother Julius had abdicated the throne, Sebastian was crown prince and heir apparent. If he actually let them do this to him.

He looked down at the young woman he'd decked and swore softly, his heart doing a quick stutter. She *had* to be okay. If she was seriously injured...

"I'm not dead," she murmured suddenly, though her eyes didn't open.

His heart lurched in relief. She could talk. *Thank God*, he said silently, but aloud he was less reverential.

"Then why are you pretending?" he asked, not really keeping the exasperation from his voice.

"I'm not pretending," she said drowsily. "I'm resting."

Sitting back on his heels, he stared at her. "Strange place for a sudden nap," he noted dryly.

She opened large blue eyes at that, eyes that widened at the sight of his bare, muscular chest, jerked up to meet his gaze, then quickly snapped shut again.

"Too much, too soon," she muttered softly,

snuggling down under the towel as if she were holding the world at bay.

Her words were barely audible and he frowned. She wasn't making any sense.

"What was that?" he said sharply.

She didn't respond. She was lying so still he could almost believe he'd imagined her talking a moment before.

He wanted to run his hands over her, looking for injuries, but he was fairly sure she wouldn't accept that without protest. And he couldn't blame her. After all, if he found an injury, what was he going to do about it? Better to wait for Will, who was supposed to know what he was doing in this arena.

At least her color was returning. She was beginning to look less like an accident victim and more like a perfectly healthy young woman. No visible signs of harm. So why was she just lying there?

Women. Who could figure them out under the best of circumstances? Luckily, for most of his life he hadn't had to. Women came and went like the weather—a different type for every season. Very early he had learned to keep his emotions out of relationships. That way he didn't have to try to analyze motivations. When you didn't expect much, you didn't feel shortchanged.

Still, she wasn't bad to look at. He'd never seen her before, but he assumed she worked here in the castle—and as he hadn't been around lately, he no longer knew all the staff. She seemed small and defenseless, all rounded corners, no sharp edges. No makeup, either, which made her seem awfully young at first glance. A second glance revealed a young woman in her late twenties. Honey-colored hair curled around a face that was pretty in a girl-next-door sort of way.

Not his type, though. Not at all.

"Listen, you're going to have to communicate with me," he ordered firmly. "I've got to know if you're badly hurt."

She stirred.

"Hurt?"

Opening her eyes again, she risked another quick look in his direction, her face scrunched up in bewilderment. Then she looked around as though she'd forgotten where she was.

"Wait a minute. Where am I? What happened?"

She didn't remember? That seemed odd. Despite her claim to be resting, she'd obviously been stunned. He supposed a blow to the head could knock the memory center for a loop—but hopefully it was just temporary.

"You're at the indoor castle swimming pool

where you very inconveniently placed yourself in the path of a stray water-polo ball," he told her lightly. "Next time, I advise you to duck."

Her gaze settled on him and her eyes narrowed suspiciously. "I see," she said, her hand going to her head, probing for lumps. "And who threw this stray ball?"

He ignored the sudden unaccustomed flash of guilt. "To tell you the truth, I guess *I* did."

She blinked as though trying to figure something out and he realized her mind still wasn't really clear.

"Were you aiming at me?" she asked, her voice slightly slurred.

His wide mouth twisted. "If I'd been aiming at you, the ball wouldn't have bounced first."

The look of bewilderment deepened and he quickly added, "No, of course I wasn't aiming at you. I was trying to shoot around a defender and the shot got away from me."

"So it was an accident."

"Of course."

She nodded and closed her eyes again.

"Actually, it feels so good to just lie here," she murmured drowsily. "I'm so-o-o tired. I haven't slept for days."

Neither had he, for that matter. Ever since he'd

been told to wrap up his affairs and head back to Meridia to prepare for his own coronation, sleep had been elusive at best.

He'd flown in to Chadae, the capital where his ancestral castle stood, only a couple of hours before. Hitching a ride on a friend's private jet had allowed him to arrive unheralded and given him the time to unwind with a short water-polo game before facing his uncle and the rest of the council.

"What's your name?" he asked her gruffly.

"Emma. Emma Valentine."

She was peeking at him from beneath thick eyelashes. He stared right back at her.

"Do you work here at the castle?"

"Sort of. I'm a chef. But I just arrived last night."

Pacio came skidding back into the pool area as she spoke and Sebastian noticed she closed her eyes more tightly instead of looking up to see what was going on. She still seemed to want to ward off reality. He wondered what she was afraid of.

"Hey, Monty," Pacio cried, calling Sebastian by the nickname, short for Dumontier, often used for him. He was grinning and motioning toward the scene he saw, with Emma still stretched out before the prince. "This is just like *Sleeping Beauty*. Maybe all she needs is a kiss from…"

Sebastian shot him a quelling look before he'd finished that sentence and cut him off with a demand.

"Where's the doctor?"

Pacio stopped short and shrugged. "We can't find him."

Sebastian thought for a moment. "Have you checked the stables?"

"No, we—"

"Try the stables. You can call down there from the hall phone."

"Okay." Pacio paused, looking down at Emma, then grinned and made a kissing motion, but Sebastian shot back a murderous look that had him hurrying away again.

He turned back to the limp figure on the shiny tile. Her breathing seemed a bit shallow to him.

"Are you falling asleep?" he asked her, incredulous.

"Just a little," she murmured softly. "I'm so sleepy. Just let me sleep."

Staring down at her, he wasn't sure if he was annoyed or amused.

"I don't think you should do that. You should probably keep talking."

"I don't want to talk. You talk." She pulled the towel up around her shoulders, then opened one eye just a bit to look at him. "Tell me a story," she suggested sleepily. "I'll bet you're good at that. You're the type."

He looked at her sharply, wondering if she was more aware than he'd thought. Maybe he was being thin-skinned, but her comment sounded like derision to him.

"I think I resent that."

She shrugged. "It's a free country."

"Meridia?" he muttered cynically. "What gives you that idea?"

She didn't answer but he hadn't meant her to. He had mixed feelings about his native country. A love-hate relationship of sorts. Meridia was his home and now his legacy. But it was also a place that had deeply damaged too many in his family—a place where his father had died under suspicious circumstances. A place that now wanted him as king.

"When are you going to start?" she asked.

He turned, looking down at her. "Start what?"

"Telling stories."

He stared at her, wondering if she was always this strange or if he'd caused it. "Do you seriously expect me to sit here and tell you stories?"

"Sure. Why not? We're in a castle, aren't we? Fairy tales would seem to be in order."

"Have you been drinking?" he asked suddenly as the possibility occurred to him.

"Just the cooking sherry," she shot back, then giggled. "Only kidding. No, I have not been drinking. But I'm feeling kind of...I don't know... kind of punchy." She gazed at him through squinted eyelids. "Can getting hit on the head make you punchy?"

He shrugged. "We'll ask Will when he gets here. If he ever gets here."

She frowned, shading her eyes as she looked up at him. "Who is Will?"

"The castle medical man."

She winced, then yawned. "I don't need a doctor. I just need a better place to sleep."

"And I'm pretty sure I'm going to need a good stiff drink myself before this is over," he muttered. "I might even settle for the cooking sherry. I've settled for worse."

He sank back against a post and tried to get comfortable on the hard floor. Every sound in the high-ceilinged pool area echoed against the walls, every lap of water against tile, every drip, giving the place an eerie, spooky feel. He supposed he could dispel that with the sound of his own voice, but he didn't want to do that. There was no way in hell he was going to tell her a story. He might go so far as to give her a nudge with his foot if she seemed to be drifting off. Other than that, they would wait for Will.

Emma was racing through a thick forest, dodging trees. That shimmering white vision she'd just barely glimpsed had to be a unicorn. She had to find it. There! Wasn't that it? She ran faster. You had to be clever to catch a unicorn and now she was tiring, her breath searing her throat. Just a little further. It had to be there. Just beyond that huge ragged trunk...her feet were like stones and the unicorn's hot breath was on her neck and...

Only it wasn't that at all, it was a strong male hand on her shoulder and it felt divine. She looked up. It was that tall, handsome man again, the one with the incredible tan and the golden chest hair and the muscles that curled and swelled like waves on a Mediterranean sea. Was she still dreaming? He was really too good to be true.

His face was strong, his features even, and he had the most beautiful golden eyes she'd ever seen. His hair was naturally dark but the ends had been bleached out by the sun, giving him a sort of golden halo effect. That, along with the dark tan, gave mute testimony to a life spent outdoors—either doing manual labor or lazing about at seaside resorts. She had a feeling she knew which it might be.

He was the sort of man women called "hot" and for the first time in her life she thought she really understood what that meant. His touch left tingles behind. She wanted to have that feeling again.

Men like this never paid much attention to girls like her, but she supposed he was only trying to be nice since he'd been the one to knock her down. What would it be like to slip into his arms and hold that beautiful body close to hers? Just thinking of it made her pulse begin to beat a rhythm at the base of her throat. He was looking at her strangely. She had a moment of quick panic—could he read her mind?

No, probably not.

But why did he keep waking her up? She was so tired and it was so hot and humid in this place and she only wanted to close her eyes and let the world go away.

But there was someone else here now. He was testing her out, checking for injuries. His touch didn't have the same electric charge as the other one, but it had a certain confident comfort to it and she didn't protest as he examined just about everything there was to examine on her.

"Good lord, Monty," the new man was saying,

teasing. "I'd heard you were losing it. But I didn't know you'd gotten to the point of having to knock a woman down and drag her off just to get a date."

Emma had to struggle to open her eyes and see who the newcomer was. But he was worth the effort—a dark-haired, handsome man in riding clothes, bearing a small black bag and looking down at her kindly.

"I didn't knock her down," the even more handsome man who'd been staying with her all this time and whose name seemed to be Monty was saying defensively. "Well, not exactly…"

"I heard she got hit by a water-polo ball," the new man said, slipping a blood-pressure cuff up her arm and starting to pump. "A water-polo ball that you threw. I'd call that a knock-down."

"We've already established the guilt in this situation," Monty responded acerbically. "But the motives were pure."

He leaned toward her. "Emma, this irritating man is Dr Will Harris. He'll get to the bottom of this 'resting' business." He nodded toward the doctor. "Will, this is Emma Valentine. She can't seem to stop sleeping. Maybe you can find out why."

"Emma Valentine, ay? Pretty name." Will smiled at her. "Pretty name for a pretty lady." He released the pressure and began to take her pulse. "What do you do here at the castle, Emma?"

She blinked at him, then closed her eyes and searched her mind. The facts seemed to have slipped away. What *was* she doing here, anyway?

"She says she's a chef." Monty answered for her. "I didn't know we were hiring chefs. But then, I don't know much about what's going on here these days."

"Yes, I was surprised to see you back so soon," the doctor said as he pulled the cuff back off again and took out his stethoscope. "Raring to go, I imagine."

Monty gave a short, humorless laugh. "Hardly that."

"Something told me you might not be completely enthusiastic with the changes around here. But I assume you will do what's expected of you. Right?"

The silence that followed seemed ripe with an emotion she couldn't understand, but it did seem to spur her memory.

"I've been hired for a special job," she said suddenly and in a surprisingly loud voice.

She smiled. What a relief to have that information back where she could retrieve it. She needed to wake up. She *had* to wake up. It was her first day on this job and she couldn't afford to blow it. She had to get herself together, enforce some self-discipline. But her eyelids were so heavy. Struggling, she opened her eyes and turned so that she could see them both.

"The coronation celebration dinners," she added. "I'm here to plan for the big event."

"Oh. That."

She noted the two men give each other a meaningful look but she couldn't imagine why and she went on.

"I came, actually, to meet with the prince. You know, the one who's going to be crowned?" She thought for a moment, then brightened. "Prince Sebastian. That's his name. And now they tell me he won't be here until the weekend."

"They told me the same thing," the doctor said with a grin she didn't think she was awake enough to analyze.

"Never trust anything 'they' tell you," Monty offered cynically. He wasn't grinning but he caught her eye and gave her a significant look, too. She had no idea why, and she frowned at him.

"They told me Agatha was coming as well," Will said with studied disinterest. "Any truth to that rumor?"

"Could be," Monty replied. "I haven't talked to her."

She was half sitting now, while Dr Will checked out her breathing, thumping her chest and listening intently. The entire situation felt so odd and the cavernous space with the gentle lapping of the water in the background only made it more so. She was in a castle, sitting beside an indoor swimming pool and being carefully examined by two of the most attractive men she'd ever seen. It was enough to turn a girl's head.

But she had to keep hers right where it was. She had a job to do. She had to keep reminding herself of that.

"So what's he like, anyway?" she asked them.

They both stared at her.

"Who?" they said at the same time.

"The prince."

"Ah." Will laughed softly as he put away his stethoscope. "The *crown* prince, now."

"The prince?" Monty chimed in, eyes shining with what she took as amusement. "He's a fine fellow. One of the best you'll ever meet. The toast of the nation."

Will snorted, but he went on.

"I'm sure songs will be written about him soon," he said in a tone she thought might be a bit sarcastic, though she wasn't certain she was reading him right. "Stories told, legends taken down. After all, he comes from a long line of kings, and he fits the part, if you ask me. Tall as an Alpine cedar, honest as a cloistered nun, strong as a...as a..."

"A blue ox?" Will put in helpfully.

Monty gave him a baleful look.

"Strong as a northern wind, sharp as a..."

"Serpent's tooth," Will interjected. "And just as yellow."

He leaned toward her earnestly. "Don't listen to Monty. Truth be told, the prince is an ugly bloke. His eyes are small and evil and much too close together for comfort. And he's got bad breath and he's a bit of a drooler, if you know what I mean."

"Really?" Emma was pretty sure he wasn't being serious. Despite the fact that her mind was still full of cotton, she was alert enough to know when her leg was being pulled. "I'd heard he was quite handsome."

"Who told you that?" Monty asked with interest.

But Will waved it away. "They always say that about royalty. You know the media. Always trying to hype their main product. They give royals attributes they don't deserve, just to make them more interesting to the public."

Emma frowned. "I don't know if that's true." Her face cleared. "Oh, you're teasing. I know he's very handsome. I don't think I've ever seen pictures myself—I don't really follow the society pages. But I've heard it from others, people who pay attention to these things. I'm sure he's quite good-looking."

"Well, don't you believe it," the doctor said cheerfully as he packed away his instruments. "I know him personally. Lazy layabout, that's what he is. Never done a day's worth of work in his life. Always off on some yacht in the Mediterranean or the Caribbean."

"Isn't that pretty much the way they all are, those royals?" Emma asked him, looking for confirmation. "At least, from what I hear."

Monty scowled but Will nodded wisely. "Over-endowed libido, under-endowed intellect," he noted. "That's our boy, the prince. Take my word for it."

Monty's head swung around at that and his mouth opened in protest. "Hey!"

"Yes, my dear," Will droned on. "Centuries of inbreeding." He made a face. "Leaves them a little bewildered, you know. You'll catch a glimpse of one now and then wandering mournfully about the castle like a lost sheep."

"That does it," Monty said, springing lightly to his feet and lunging for the doctor. "You're going into the pool."

CHAPTER TWO

EMMA gasped, feeling dizzy. She was used to verbal rages between people. They happened all the time in her very volatile family. But physical confrontations were different. Were these two very large men actually going to fight?

Monty's body seemed to be a symphony of muscles all working together taking a form a Greek statue would have envied. His legs looked like steel and his arms bulged in places she hadn't known she liked to see bulges. And the sense she got of things barely covered by that tiny black swimsuit made her blush and suddenly, to her surprise, she had to catch her breath.

But she couldn't tear her gaze away. Monty was just so beautiful. The only flaw seemed to be a long ridged scar from just beneath his ribs down toward his hip-bone, as though a knife had…

She shuddered, not wanting to think what might have made it. And at the same moment

Monty grimaced and seemed to clutch at the scar area.

Will stopped wrestling immediately. "That still bothering you?" he asked, frowning.

Monty shrugged, straightening slowly. "It grabs now and then. Mostly it's okay," he said dismissively. "It doesn't stop me from doing much."

Still, it was obvious that the so-called fight was truly over.

"You ought to get the scar tissue massaged periodically," Will told him. "It's probably building up calcium deposits. A little massage with Vitamin E should help break it down again."

Monty nodded, rubbing the scar with his hand as though that were relieving pain. "If it hadn't been for this, you'd be in the pool by now," he said, threatening his friend mockingly.

Will grinned and turned to Emma.

"It's touching how protective he is of the prince," he explained to her as he held off the other man's by now half-hearted attack. "I'm afraid I take a more realistic view."

"Your view of everything will be quite damp if you keep it up," Sebastian warned him. "You got off easy this time."

Will didn't look particularly chastened, but he did glance at the pool, then grinned at his friend.

"Okay, you win. No more about the prince. I've got doctor stuff to do. Let me talk to the young lady, if you please."

Monty let him go with some reluctance, glared at him a moment longer, then stood back and made a sweeping bow. "Be my guest."

Emma sighed with relief as Will stepped around him rather gingerly, then smiled at his patient. Even though their entire battle had had the choreographed look of something they had done many times before, probably beginning in childhood, she was glad it was over.

And she was glad it was Will who was coming to her side. There was something nice and comforting about the doctor. She was pretty sure she was going to like him.

Monty, on the other hand, was beginning to make her distinctly uncomfortable. There was something sharp and edgy about him. He was nice to look at, but in a hard, scary way that disturbed her. His golden eyes seemed to see too much and to scorn much of what he saw. His full, beautifully defined lips seemed to stretch more often in disdain than in smiling. There was a ruthless, wild quality in him, something she'd first noticed when he was wrestling with Will. She suddenly thought of what he reminded her of—an untamed horse, a stallion that was beautiful to watch, but frightening to get too close to.

"Well, Emma, your vital signs seem normal. You've got a lump on your scalp. I assume it marks the spot where you hit the ground rather than where the ball hit you. Either way, it's a rather simple scalp trauma and you've sustained a bit of a concussion. You'll need to be checked on over the next twenty-four hours."

She nodded. That seemed to fit with her picture of what was going on here.

"I don't see anything especially serious. However, your lethargic reaction is a bit troubling. Before making a diagnosis, I always like to ask the patient himself what he…or she… thinks has brought something like this on. What do you think might have caused it?"

She shrugged. "Overwork, I guess. Lack of sleep. Stress."

He frowned. "What are you doing that might be causing all this stress?"

That was an easy one. Ever since she'd been offered this contract, she'd been obsessed with every detail, working as hard as she ever had in her life to make sure she came through and didn't embarrass herself, her restaurant, or—most of all—her father.

And there was more, of course. It had been a crazy summer so far, with her beloved grandfather William dying in June. Because of strained relations with her own father and a schizophrenic connection with her mother, she'd clung to the older man at times, soaking up his love and responding in kind. His death had been natural, but a sorrowful one for his huge extended family. His sad funeral had been a sort of reunion for the remaining Valentine clan, conjuring up all sorts of emotions that had been papered over for years. With so much going on, sometimes she felt as though she were running at full scream level without the sound.

But she couldn't tell him all of that. Much easier to keep it simple.

"My job," she said, nodding confidently. "I've been staying up late preparing for this special assignment for weeks now. I work all day as chef at a restaurant in London and study half the night. Then when I finally do go to bed, my heart is still racing like a hamster on his little wheel, running faster and faster. I don't seem to be able to slow down again."

"So the more tired you get, the less you sleep."

"It seems that way."

"Yet you had no trouble falling asleep on this hard tile floor."

She crinkled her nose, thinking. "It was...pleasant. Sort of like taking a vacation from real life, lying here with my eyes closed." She managed a weak smile. "I started to think a little temporary coma might be nice."

He shook his head. "No comas. You might start liking them too much."

He was right. She needed to get back into reality. Gathering all her strength, she sat up fully.

"Hey, take it easy," Will said, reaching out to steady her.

And there it was again, that deep, provocative tingle that made her gasp. The man's hands were like magic. Black magic. There was something in his touch that tempted her to curl herself into his arms, inviting more, but she stopped herself quickly, hoping he hadn't noticed her reaction—or her automatic recoil once she'd realized what was happening.

"I'm fine, really." She looked up into his face, then away again quickly. "Just...just a little woozy."

Will nodded, thinking for a moment. "I don't want to give you anything—no pills, no shots. In my experience, things like that often create more new problems while hardly dealing with the old ones. I leave the drugs to last resort." He paused.

"What I would like is for you to take a nice long nap," he said at last, looking into her eyes gravely.

"I'd like that too," she said, feeling a little as though she might cry if she didn't watch it. Emotions were bubbling inside her and she didn't have the strength to try to sort them out as yet. "But I can't. I've got to get back to work. I just went off for a walk to find a cooler place than the kitchen for a bit. I'm sure they all wonder what on earth happened to me. Especially the housekeeper."

"I'll let them know." Will started to help her to her feet. "I'm going to take you to your room. Doctor's orders."

Monty rose as well. "I'll come too."

She started to shake her head, horrified, but Will beat her to it.

"No, you won't. You can't wander around the castle in your swimsuit like you do on your yachts. There are sensibilities to be considered. Maids will be fainting in the halls."

"That's ridiculous."

But Will was serious. "Monty, you're not who you used to be. You have a new position and you've got to maintain some decorum."

Emma wasn't sure what they were talking about, but she knew she wanted to get away from

Monty and his cool gaze as soon as possible. She could tell he was bristling.

"So now you're ordering me around?" he said coldly to his friend.

Will nodded. "I'm sure you'll give me this much leeway," he said softly. "For old times' sake."

Monty stared at him for a long moment, then shrugged and turned to Emma. "Where's your room?" he asked her.

Her eyes widened. "I have no idea. I get lost every time I turn a corner in this place."

"How are you going to find it again if you don't know where it is?"

"Someone will tell us," Will said.

"It's very high up," Emma added, trying to be helpful. "A nice room. The sort of place that feels like if they locked me in and I grew my hair long…"

"Rapunzel, Rapunzel?" Monty's look of irritation stung. "There you go with the fairy tales again." His gaze raked over her. "All right, go with Will. I'll check on you later."

"Monty…" Will began in a warning tone.

"You can keep your opinions to yourself," Monty ordered, giving his friend a look that registered something close to disgust. "You don't have to worry. She's clearly not my type at all."

Will made a scoffing sound in his throat. "She's female, isn't she?" he said softly, plainly not meaning the comment for Emma to hear.

But she'd heard all right, and her mind had cleared enough to know that she wanted to avoid a room visit from this man at all costs.

"You don't need to worry about me," she said quickly, stepping a bit closer to Will. "The doctor will handle it."

He stared at her and she realized she'd been a little too obvious in her anxiety. No emotion showed in his eyes, but she could feel his hostility.

"As you wish," he said evenly. "Goodbye, Emma Valentine."

Reaching out, he took her hand and bent from the waist to brush her fingers with his lips. "Until we meet again."

He left her breathless but at least he was gone.

"What did he do that for?" she asked Will as they started toward the castle elevator. Her hand was tingling and she rubbed it against her shorts.

"He likes to keep us all on our toes by doing the unexpected," Will told her cheerfully.

He'd certainly fulfilled that image today, she thought with some irritation.

"You're the castle physician," she said to the doctor. "What does Monty do?"

"Monty?" He chuckled. "You might say Monty is a servant to us all."

She frowned, wishing she could really get rid of all the cobwebs so she could understand better what was going on around her. "What is that supposed to mean?"

"All in due time, my dear. All in due time."

She was lost. Again.

"They should hand out maps at the door of this place," she muttered in frustration as she hurried down one hall and then up another, hoping to see something familiar—anything at all.

It would also have helped if there had been someone to ask for directions, but the halls she went racing down were empty. Maybe she was lost in a ghost castle.

But she knew better. It had only been a half-hour before that she'd had a visit from Myrna Luk, the castle housekeeper.

"Well, he's done it again," she'd said as she breezed into Emma's room. A pretty woman in her late forties, she seemed harried and over-worked but managed to keep a friendly look on her face, which was more than most of the staff had welcomed Emma with.

"Who's done what?" Emma asked, reaching

for her white uniform, anxious to show that she was ready to join in after having been AWOL for so long. She'd had a wonderful long nap and was feeling very much herself again. Dr Will had been to check on her and had been pleased with her condition. So things were looking up.

"The prince, of course. Prince Sebastian." The housekeeper put a hand up to smooth down the curls of her dark brown hair. "He's here, crept in on us unannounced. The level of service for dinner will have to be raised. It won't just be the duke and the duchess. It will be the prince as well." She began counting out diners on her fingers. "And the Italian ambassador, so they tell me, along with his wife and sister. The chancellor of the treasury, the minister of defense and his wife. And of course, Romas, the old duke's son, and…let's see…"

"The prince is here?"

Emma was suddenly nervous. She'd been ready to meet the prince and begin working out menus with him, but when they had told her he wouldn't arrive until the weekend she'd been disappointed, but secretly a little relieved. That gave her a little more time. And now he was here after all, and she didn't feel prepared.

"Yes, he's here. And us being so shorthanded.

So the chef tells me." The housekeeper looked at Emma speculatively. "I know it's not what you're here for but you might as well pitch in. After all, you need to get the lay of the land and see how things are done around here. So…do you mind working with Chef Henri?"

"No. No, of course not."

Emma was amenable but she wondered how Chef Henri would take it. When she'd met the man the night before she'd had the distinct impression he would have liked to see her filleted along with the fish course. Actually, she'd come face to face with a wall of hostility from most of the kitchen staff. It had been evident right away that they greatly resented that she'd been chosen as chef to the coronation over someone home-grown.

"You look a little tired," Myrna Luk was saying. "And Dr Will filled me in on your situation. Sure you're up to this?"

"Oh, absolutely."

Regardless of how she felt, she *had* to be up to it. After all, this was the housekeeper, the only person on the staff who had actually been nice to her so far, asking for help. If she couldn't come through for her, she might as well give up and go home.

"How are you getting on?" Myrna asked, looking her over a bit more closely.

Emma hesitated, tempted to tell her the truth—that the staff was treating her like a redheaded stepchild. But what, after all, was that going to get her—except more antagonism from them? Anyway, this was her job and she had to take care of it herself.

"Quite fine, thank you."

"Wonderful. Then I'll tell Chef Henri that you're willing."

"Yes."

Willing, surely. But able? That remained to be seen.

Though she was refreshed from the best sleep she'd had in a week, she still hadn't gone over what had happened that morning and come to terms with it. That would have to come later. Right now, she needed to find that darn elevator, or maybe some stairs, and get to the kitchen.

She turned a corner and there it was. The ancient elevator. Sighing with relief, she hurried up and pushed the button. The elevator lumbered toward her with much creaking and clashing of metal against metal, giving her qualms. And then the doors slid open.

"Oh, no!"

The reaction slipped out before she could stop it, for there stood the very man she most wanted to avoid seeing again.

He didn't look any happier to see her.

"Well, come on, get on board," he said gruffly. "I won't bite." One eyebrow rose. "Though I might nibble a little," he added, mostly to amuse himself.

But she wasn't paying any attention to what he was saying. She was staring at him, taking in the royal-blue uniform he was wearing, with gold braid and glistening badges decorating the sleeves, epaulettes and upright collar. Ribbons and medals covered the breast of the short, fitted jacket. A gold-encrusted sabre hung at his side. And suddenly it was clear to her who this man really was.

She gulped wordlessly. Reaching out, he took her elbow and pulled her aboard. The doors slid closed. And finally she found her tongue.

"You...you're the prince."

He nodded, barely glancing at her. "Yes. Of course."

She raised a hand and covered her mouth for a moment. "I should have known."

"Of course you should have. I don't know why you didn't." He punched the ground-floor button to get the elevator moving again, then turned to look down at her. "A relatively bright five-year-old child would have tumbled to the truth right away."

Her shock faded as her indignation at his tone asserted itself. He might be the prince, but he was still just as annoying as he had been earlier that day.

"A relatively bright five-year-old child without a bump on the head from a badly thrown water-polo ball, maybe," she said defensively. She wasn't feeling woozy any longer and she wasn't about to let him bully her, no matter how royal he was. "I was unconscious half the time."

"And just clueless the other half, I guess," he said, looking bemused.

The arrogance of the man was really galling.

"I suppose you think your 'royalness' is so obvious it sort of shimmers around you for all to see?" she challenged. "Or, better yet, oozes from your pores like...like sweat on a hot day?"

"Something like that," he acknowledged calmly. "Most people tumble to it pretty quickly. In fact, it's hard to hide even when I want to avoid dealing with it."

"Poor baby," she said, still resenting his manner. "I guess that works better with injured people who are half asleep." Looking at him, she felt a strange emotion she couldn't identify. It was as though she wanted to prove something to him, but she wasn't sure what. "And anyway, you know you did your best to fool me," she added.

His brows knit together as though he really didn't know what she was talking about. "I didn't do a thing."

"You told me your name was Monty."

"It is." He shrugged. "I have a lot of names. Some of them are too rude to be spoken to my face, I'm sure." He glanced at her sideways, his hand on the hilt of his sabre. "Perhaps you're contemplating one of those right now."

You bet I am.

That was what she would like to say. But it suddenly occurred to her that she was supposed to be working for this man. If she wanted to keep the job of coronation chef, maybe she'd better keep her opinions to herself. So she clamped her mouth shut, took a deep breath, and looked away, trying hard to calm down.

The elevator ground to a halt and the doors slid open laboriously. She moved to step forward, hoping to make her escape, but his hand shot out again and caught her elbow.

"Wait a minute. *You're* a woman," he said, as though that thought had just presented itself to him.

"That's a rare ability for insight you have there, Your Highness," she snapped before she could stop herself. And then she winced. She was going to have to do better than that if she was going to keep this relationship on an even keel.

But he was ignoring her dig. Nodding, he stared at her with a speculative gleam in his golden eyes. "I've been looking for a woman, but you'll do."

She blanched, stiffening. "I'll do for what?"

He made a head gesture in a direction she knew was opposite of where she was going and his grip tightened on her elbow.

"Come with me," he said abruptly, making it an order.

She dug in her heels, thinking fast. She didn't much like orders. "Wait! I can't. I have to get to the kitchen."

"Not yet. I need you."

"You what?" Her breathless gasp of surprise was soft, but she knew he'd heard it.

"I need you," he said firmly. "Oh, don't look so shocked. I'm not planning to throw you into the hay and have my way with you. I need you for something a bit more mundane than that."

She felt color rushing into her cheeks and she silently begged it to stop. Here she was, formless and stodgy in her chef's whites. No makeup, no stiletto heels. Hardly the picture of the *femme fatale* he was undoubtedly used to. The likelihood that he would have any carnal interest in her was remote at best. To have him think she was hysterically defending her virtue was humiliating.

"Well, what if I don't want to go with you?" she said in hopes of deflecting his attention from her blush.

"Too bad."

"What?"

Amusement sparkled in his eyes. He was certainly enjoying this. And that only made her more determined to resist him.

"I'm the prince, remember? And we're in the castle. My orders take precedence. It's that old pesky divine rights thing."

Her jaw jutted out. Despite her embarrassment, she couldn't let that pass.

"Over my free will? Never!"

Exasperation filled his face.

"Hey, call out the historians. Someone will write a book about you and your courageous principles." His eyes glittered sardonically. "But in the meantime, Emma Valentine, you're coming with me."

CHAPTER THREE

EMMA glared at Sebastian. It wasn't enough that he was arrogant and bossy—he thought he could mock her principles, too. She'd about had it with this man. Prince or no prince, he had a lesson in manners due him.

Her half-sister Rachel had warned her about this prince just a few days ago. Emma had been staying with Rachel and her new husband at their French vineyard. As she'd been packing up for her flight to Meridia Rachel had come in and flopped down on the bed.

"Be careful," she said. "You know what these young royals are like these days. And I hear this one's a perfect example of a playboy."

"Really?" That wasn't the first time Emma had heard that, but she didn't think it was going to affect her work. "I doubt I'll even meet with him more than once," she assured her sister.

Rachel pursed her lips and gazed at her speculatively. "That's probably for the best," she said slowly. "It might be just as well if you didn't get your pretty little head turned."

Emma sighed. "Don't."

"What's the matter?"

"Rachel, you know I've never been pretty. Competent, yes. Smart. Quick. Good at my job. But never pretty."

Rachel stared at her, aghast. "What are you talking about? You're gorgeous. Emma Valentine, I'll bet you haven't looked in a mirror since you were sixteen."

Emma raised her head. "I'm looking in the mirror right now."

"And you see a lovely woman hidden behind hair that you didn't bother to brush this morning and a naturally lovely face with no mascara to draw attention to your beautiful blue eyes."

"Oh, please. I have no intention of trying to be a seductress here."

"I know, but that's not the point. A little evidence that you might be open to some male attention is all I'm asking for."

"But I'm not."

Rachel rolled her eyes. "Okay. We'll talk about this later. After the Meridia gig. The last thing I would want to do would be to encourage a prince to start chasing you."

The whole concept had made her laugh. And it was still ridiculous to contemplate. This prince was certainly gorgeous, but he was as arrogant and unpleasant as they came.

"Listen, mister," she began, trying to pull away from his grip on her elbow. "The divine rights of kings is all very well. Just don't forget about *noblesse oblige*."

"Emma, *you* listen," he said, giving every sign of a man who'd also come to the end of his patience. "I told you I need a woman's touch. And you're that woman."

She looked up into his eyes and what she saw there gave her shivers. Was he really that cold-hearted? Or was this just a royal trait?

"But, I need to get to the kitchen," she tried, knowing the weakness of her voice was giving away the fact that her stand had weakened, too.

"Calm down." His mouth twitched at the corners as he waited a moment for her to breathe evenly again, then he gestured toward his collar where a coil of braid flapped out, flying loose. "I just need a bit of repair work. A little sewing. That's all."

For the first time, she noticed that he held a needle and a long tail of thread in his other hand.

"I can't sew," she said quickly.

"Liar." Now he was laughing at her. "If you took cooking classes, I have no doubt a sewing lesson or two lurked in there somewhere. Come on. You're going to sew this braid back on for me."

"But—"

"Emma, have a heart. I've got to get to the reception in the entry hall. They're waiting for me. And I can't show up like this." He paused, and then, with what seemed like a lot of effort, he made himself say, "Please."

She bristled, and then slowly relaxed. There was no point in keeping up this resistance when she knew she was going to have to give in eventually anyway. And if all he really wanted was a bit of needlework, the more quickly she got to it, the more quickly she would be back on her way to the kitchen. Besides, she was a sucker for people who said "please".

"Oh, all right," she said, shaking her head in resignation. "I'll give it a try. But I'm warning you, I'm not very good at it."

He nodded and led her into a small room just a few feet away from the elevator. It seemed to be a storage center of sorts, with maps pinned and glued all over the walls and large pieces of luggage stacked on shelves and set about in piles.

"We'll be out of the way here," he said, dropping down to sit on a tall stool and handing her the needle. "Sew like the wind, my sweet, and we'll be back on our way in no time."

She put a knot in the thread rather absently as she looked down at his collar. He'd unbuttoned the top buttons so that it could be pulled to the side a bit. The braid was definitely loose, and somewhat shredded in places, but she knew she could take care of it easily. Still…

She cleared her throat nervously. "You know, this would be a lot easier to do if you took the jacket off," she suggested.

He shook his head. "Can't do it. You don't know what it cost me to get into this damn monkey suit in the first place. I'll never be able to summon the patience to do it again."

She sighed. Nothing was ever completely easy, was it? "Hold still, then."

Her fingers were shaking. She bit her lip, trying to stop them. If she couldn't keep steady and the needle slipped… She winced, thinking of it. He'd have her fired for sure.

Fired! Hah! Killed, more likely.

She almost laughed aloud and somehow that thought steadied her. Taking a deep breath, she pressed the piece of braid down where it evidently belonged and began her first probe with the needle.

There. That wasn't so hard. She took a tiny stitch, then another, and then she was moving along as though she really did know what she was doing. The trick was going to be to keep her mind off the fact that she was doing this for the prince.

The prince! The man who was going to be King of Meridia. She hadn't let that fact sink in yet. She couldn't think about it if she was going to get through this task alive.

But it wasn't easy. She had to force herself to ignore the sense of his body heat that wafted up from his open-necked uniform, bringing with it a clean, masculine scent. Her fingers brushed the warm skin of his neck every now and then. And she felt a sensation—a sort of flutter of excitement—every time.

It was only natural. After all, he was a very attractive man—smooth skin, thick, shiny hair, and the most beautiful ear... Her mouth was dry and she was embarrassed. But, after all, she wouldn't be human if all that didn't affect her— just a little.

And she knew it didn't mean a thing. He was as self-centered as they came. And, more than that, he was dangerous. She didn't want to spell out just exactly what he threatened in her. Better not to think about that. But she'd known enough to shy away from him even before she'd found out he was the prince. She just had to keep that in mind.

The most ridiculous thing in the world would be to let herself get a crush on this man. But she really didn't fear that because she wasn't the type to get caught up in romance. It had never been all that important to her. She'd been too busy becoming the best chef she could be. So she wasn't really very worried.

Still, if love was a contagious disease, she ought to get a vaccination. Just recently her half-sisters, the twins, Rebecca and Rachel, had both come down with it. Emma had celebrated Rebecca's marriage in Wyoming, then stopped to visit Rachel and her new husband, Luc, at their vineyard in France before coming to Meridia.

It was wonderful that both her older sisters had found love the way they had. But it did exact its own sort of toll on her spirit. She'd never been in love herself—never had time. She was almost thirty. Was it too late for her to find a way to develop the knack for it? If it hadn't happened in all this time, maybe it never would.

That was a disturbing thought and, added to the jumble that was now her emotional life—just another thing she didn't have time to think about.

The sound of a voice from down the hall made her realize it had been some time since either of them had spoken. It was almost beginning to feel awkward. She tried to think of something to say, but how did you strike up a conversation with a prince?

Still, this wasn't just any prince. This was the man who'd knocked her out with a water-polo ball, then sat with her while she'd tried to get him to tell her fairy tales. Surely she could think of something to say to him.

"So," she said tentatively, going back over some of her stitches to strengthen the hold, "you're going to be King. I guess that must be pretty thrilling."

Glancing up, he gave her a quizzical look. "I can think of other words for it," he muttered.

"Well, *I'm* thrilled," she persisted. "This is going to be my first chance to show an international audience what I can do. I only hope I do you proud."

He was looking at her as though he thought her hopelessly naïve, but she didn't care.

"I have some really unique plans. I'd like to go

over them with you when you have a minute. Maybe tomorrow morning?"

She knew she was starting to show how much she loved her work, and she also knew that such an open attitude was probably considered completely tedious in his crowd, but she couldn't pretend to be sophisticated—because she was anything but. He was the prince and she was the commoner—and she wasn't going to try to be anything else.

"Wait until you see some of the menus."

"I can hardly contain my excitement," he said dryly, and, though he didn't put that sarcastic, mocking tone he so often used in his voice, she could tell he was having trouble holding it back, and she flushed again.

Biting her lower lip, she vowed to quit trying to be polite. It didn't pay with this man. If he wasn't interested in having a normal conversation, so be it.

But then she noticed he was staring at one of the maps on the wall across from where he sat. Reaching out, he could just barely reach it. Very slowly, almost lovingly, he traced the outline of Italy with his forefinger.

"Italy's a wonderful country," she said.

He nodded but he didn't say anything.

"I was in Rome last year for an Italian meringue seminar. It was a trip I'll never forget."

He gave her a dubious look. "The Italians have their own type of meringue?" he asked.

"Oh, yes. You slowly pour hot sugar syrup over stiffly beaten egg whites and keep beating until the whole thing has cooled. It makes a much more stable meringue."

"Great. There's nothing I hate more than an unstable meringue."

He was making fun of her but she didn't react. Her mind had gone back to his tracing the outline of the map. There was something almost sad and regretful about the way he'd done it and she wondered why.

"My grandmother was Italian," she told him. "From Naples. My grandfather met her during the war."

"Really." He looked up, and for the first time his eyes seemed clear and interested. "My mother was Italian. She was born in Florence."

Their gazes met and held in a stolen moment of mutual understanding, a connection across a vast, empty plain. And then, as suddenly as it had appeared, it was gone, and he looked away.

Her heart was suddenly thumping in her chest.

Before she had time to catch her breath, he was speaking again, changing the subject.

"So, Emma Valentine. How did you get the job as my coronation food guru? I thought we usually used the in-house cook to do the dirty deed."

"I'm told you have in the past," she said quickly, hoping he hadn't noticed how she'd responded to that momentary bond between them. She couldn't seem to control her pulse or her breathing around him as it was and the whole thing was getting darned inconvenient. "But this time..."

She stopped and started again.

"Well, you see, Todd Akers, your coronation manager, is a regular at our restaurant in London. We've become friendly over the years. So when he had this fantastic assignment, he knew of my work. He contacted me and asked if I would be interested."

"And you were."

"Oh, yes. It's a chance of a lifetime for me."

He looked at her, curious. "In what way?"

"Well... As I said before, it's an opportunity to show the world what I can do. Make my reputation."

"And from that will come more offers for other coronations?" he asked skeptically. "How many can there be?"

"And other large affairs as well," she explained

quickly. "Also, cooking shows on television. Cookbook contracts. Positions in cooking schools. All sorts of things."

Including a chance that her father would finally feel that she'd made it in this profession. There was always that hope, dim as it might be. But she crinkled her nose and pushed those concerns away. She would worry about that when she was back in London.

"If all goes well," Sebastian said softly, his face taking on a strange, dreamy look.

"Of course. If I fail…" She caught her breath and shook her head firmly. "No! I won't even entertain the thought. I'm going to give you a coronation dinner fit for a king." She couldn't resist a quick grin. "So to speak."

"So to speak," he echoed, nodding. He glanced up at her again, his eyes hooded. "So you and Todd are…old friends."

He said it in a significant way that added a spin she couldn't let pass. Did he really think she'd been chosen for this job because she'd been… "friendly" with Todd? Frowning, she pulled back and stared at him.

"We are not 'old friends'."

He raised an eyebrow, searching her gaze. "New friends?"

"We're not 'friends' the way you make it sound." She pursed her lips, gazing at him. "You really are a cynical man, aren't you?"

He shrugged with a nonchalance that came naturally to him.

"It's a requirement for survival, sweetheart."

He gave his statement a Humphrey Bogart twist that almost made her smile. Almost.

Instead, she got an urge to lecture him.

No! the rational part of her warned.

Just a little lecture. For his own good.

No! Don't be crazy! What will you get out of it?

The lecture isn't for me. It's for him. And he needs it.

She waited a few seconds, but the rational side didn't seem to have an answer for that, so she took a deep breath and charged ahead.

"Since you're interested in survival," she began, carefully feeling her way at first, "I've got a tip for you. It'll make you a better monarch."

He looked suddenly wary. "Okay. Let's hear it."

She was rapidly developing a nervous twitch now that he was looking at her so intently, and wondering if it might not have been better to listen to her rational side after all, but she soldiered on.

"Requests and suggestions work better than orders," she said as firmly as she could, concentrating resolutely on her stitches. "Don't run roughshod over people, like you did with me just now. Make them want to help you by giving them the same respect you want from them."

He stared up at her, shaking his head, looking like a man who felt he was being wrongly accused. "What the hell are you talking about?"

"You." She glanced at him and then back to the sewing. "You tend to order people about as though their lives aren't as important as yours and—"

"No, I don't."

Now he was looking fierce, and his fierce look was enough to make her voice shake a little, no matter how tough she was determined to be.

"Yes, you do."

He shook his head. "And, anyway, maybe their lives aren't as important as mine."

Throwing her free hand in the air, she appealed to the heavens. "See what I mean?"

"So you want me to pretend," he said irritably, his jaw clenched. "To make nice."

Her heart was racing. She'd offended him. She probably shouldn't have brought it up. But she couldn't back down now. She lifted her chin and held her own.

"Yes, if it comes to that," she told him earnestly.

He glared at her. "You have some nerve, Emma Valentine," he said in a voice that could have cut through steel.

"I know."

He paused, staring at her, then shook his head. "Okay, Emma," he said gruffly. "I'll think about it."

"Oh." Relief flooded her system. "Well. Good." She wanted to laugh but she didn't dare ruin everything. "Hold still," she said as she tied off the knotted end. "There. You're finished."

Rising, he buttoned his jacket up to the neck and flexed his wide shoulders inside, then bent to look into a mirror.

"Good job," he said coolly. "It looks great."

She nodded, turning toward the doorway. "I'm off," she said, avoiding another last look into his eyes. "Goodbye."

"Emma." He caught her hand and held it until she turned back to face him. "Thank you very much."

She looked up in surprise. The way he said it, she had a feeling he didn't overuse that phrase.

"Let me know if there is any favor I can ever do for you," he added.

A certain warmth filled her. Was he saying this because she'd made him more aware? There was no way to tell, but she thought there was a chance her little lecture had actually done some good.

On the other hand, was that a mocking light she saw in his eyes? With a rueful smile, she turned. It was time to get away from him and his very potent sphere of influence.

But before she could escape, he reached out and stopped her again.

"Before you go, one word of advice for *you*, Miss Valentine," he said coolly, his golden eyes cynical. "When you hang around a royal castle, don't trust anyone."

She frowned. Was he trying to scare her? Or was his warning for real?

"Not even the king?" she asked.

His smile was humorless. "Especially not the king," he said.

The kitchen of Rolande Castle seemed to have a personality of its own—ancient, cavernous and crusty, with a certain medieval ambience. As Emma looked around it she could imagine knights of old stomping through, armor clanging, nabbing hunks of just-roasted meat with their swords. Modern stainless-steel appliances and other attempts at updating were overwhelmed by the dark atmosphere of centuries past lingering on. A huge arched brick fireplace took up one entire wall and the heat it generated was stifling. Large copper-bottomed pots hung everywhere.

"Chef Henri," she said, presenting herself to the chef, a pudgy man with a sense of the dramatic and a mustache that reminded her of Salvador Dalí. "The housekeeper said you could use some help tonight, so I…"

The stocky man's eyes flared with such outrage, she was stopped in her tracks and actually took a step backwards.

"I need no help," he spit out. "I let you join us as a favor to Myrna. She say you need to learn. Well, you watch me. You learn plenty."

Making a mental note to be sure to find something on the night's menu to rave about—anything to begin to chip away at the hostility that bristled from him—she beat a hasty path to the dessert station. The evening's treats were individual strawberry tortes with marzipan garnish, a dish she'd made before with award-winning results. To her relief, the pastry assistant wasn't particularly antagonistic and they soon were working well together.

The room was full of a churning mass of

people. It was lucky she was used to working in a crowd. After all, she'd been a head chef at her family restaurant for some time and a line cook for years before that. But there, the surroundings and resources were second nature to her. Here, she had to learn everything anew.

Time flew and suddenly it was the dinner hour. Not wanting to miss a thing, she left the dessert station to watch from the wings. A gong sounded and the march of the servers began. Two footmen, dressed in full livery, led the way. Each carried a tall silver scepter and wore a high brocade hat.

She followed them partway in to take a look, carefully staying to the shadows and pushing aside a heavy brocade drape to get a better view.

The dining hall was huge. The table looked big enough to launch airplanes into the sky. Heavy silver service framed delicate china encrusted with the royal family seal. The centerpieces ranging up and down the length of the table were made up of sterling silver candelabras entwined with roses. It was an impressive display.

Twenty-five to thirty people sat along the huge table. She scanned the crowd, looking for a familiar face, but couldn't see anyone, not even Dr. Will.

But the prince was there, at the center of it all.

At the moment he was engrossed in talking to the older man at his right and she felt a flash of relief that he hadn't seen her. Time to go, before he did.

As though her thoughts were being beamed straight at him, his head rose and he looked right into her eyes. She stood frozen, unable to move. Seconds suddenly stretched out seemingly lasting for ever. And then he rose, nodding toward her and gesturing to the empty seat beside him.

She shook her head. He couldn't be asking her to join him. Could he? She looked around for an escape, but one of the footmen had arrived by her side.

"Prince Sebastian requests your presence, Miss Valentine," he said smoothly, offering her his arm. "Come this way, please."

She looked at him, beseechingly. "Do I have to?"

He nodded, unsmiling. "Yes, Miss Valentine. Please."

This was a very bad idea. She knew that instinctively, and for a moment she toyed with making a run for it. What would he do? Send the dogs after her?

But no. She didn't want to make a scene. Besides, he was the boss. Maybe he wanted her to sit beside him and comment on the food, or plan a few meals, or chat about nutritional values.

Maybe. But not very likely.

She sighed. Might as well make the best of it and try to act as though she sat down with royalty every day.

"Lead on, MacDuff," she muttered, taking the footman's arm.

CHAPTER FOUR

"SEBASTIAN, your father would be so proud of you."

The prince gave his uncle a skeptical glance, wondering if he was talking about the same father *he'd* grown up with.

"My father used up all his sense of pride on my brother Julius," he said dryly. "And look how that turned out."

"Ah, yes." The Duke of Sandstrove nodded his heavy head, looking for all the world like a sage old lion. "As they say, pride goeth before a fall."

Sebastian wasn't too sure what that had to do with anything, but he let it go. Sitting at the head of the table, his uncle on one side and the ornate chair that had stood empty since his mother died on the other, he nursed a crystal goblet of scarlet wine and surveyed the people who had come to dine with him. They were all here, all the usual suspects. He'd known most of them all his life.

They had gathered to welcome him home. Or so

they said. Actually, they'd all come together to make sure he understood what was expected of him.

He understood all right. What they wanted was obedience—obedience to tradition, to the past, to the way things had always been done. And, most importantly, obedience to the group of élite courtiers, a sort of protectorate, who had taken over running the country when his father had fallen ill, and who expected to go on running things—even after Sebastian was crowned.

Too bad. They were in for a big disappointment.

That thought had barely surfaced in his mind when his gaze met Emma's across the room. Something electric flashed between them, and he thought he knew what it was—inspiration. She would be the perfect foil. Rising, he signaled a request for her to join him, then turned and spoke to a footman, who hurried over to escort her.

He saw the look of confusion and then horror on her face and he actually had a qualm, but it passed quickly and he stood waiting for her to arrive at his side.

"Miss Valentine. I'm delighted you could join us." He turned toward the table. "I know you will all be happy to welcome Miss Emma Valentine, our special coronation chef."

He didn't wait for a reply and that was a good thing, as most of the diners were slack-jawed with astonishment and likely unable to speak. The contrast between her severe white uniform and their bejewelled and beribboned attire was a stark one. They seemed as stunned as a herd of cattle that had run up against a barrier to their feed trough.

"You'll excuse the members of my future court and other assorted hangers-on for not rising to greet you, Miss Valentine," he said in a clear, firm voice making sure everyone heard. "They usually have better manners, but, tonight, I'm afraid they're a bit rusty."

He threw them all a wide, sunny smile, lingering pointedly on his cousin Romas, whose dark face was scowling. "I know they will brush up on their etiquette and be ready next time you grace us with your presence." He pulled out the empty chair at his left. "Please be seated."

"Thank you," she murmured, moving to do as he suggested, but the furious sideways glance she cast his way made him grin.

A shocked murmur went through the assembly as he helped Emma into the chair. He knew they

couldn't believe he was asking her to sit there—
his mother's chair. They were going to be surprised by a lot of things before he was finished.

"This is just crazy," Emma whispered. "What
are you doing?"

"When I figure that out," he whispered back,
leaning close as he pushed in her chair, "you'll be
the first to know."

Pasting on a bright smile, she looked up and
down the table. There wasn't a sound. Everyone
was staring at her, aghast. Chefs didn't sit down
next to princes. It wasn't done. They thought this
a scandal—and a little bit nuts. And she thor-
oughly agreed.

Uncle Trevoron, the duke, leaned toward Sebastian as he dropped back into his own ornately
carved chair.

"My boy, look closely," he whispered loudly,
eyeing her chef's whites. "She's a cook."

"Yes, Uncle, she's a cook. Todd Akers found
her in London and brought her here to prepare the
coronation dinner."

The duke cleared his throat, trying to be diplo-
matic. "That's all very well, but she's a cook."

"He's right," Emma said evenly, turning her
shoulders as though to prepare to rise. "I think I'd
better go back to the kitchen."

"Not yet."

His fingers loosely circled her wrist and she looked up into his face, startled. His gaze was cool and direct. She settled back in the chair, her pulse rate escalating. What on earth did he have in mind here?

"So nice to meet you, Miss Valentine," said a voice from across the table.

Emma looked up and met the kindly smile of a middle-aged woman with perfectly styled hair and a brown silk drapey dress that didn't quite succeed in its job of hiding her pleasingly plump figure.

"My aunt Trudy," Sebastian murmured. "Duchess of Sandstrove."

"I'm honored," Emma said, unable to hide her relief at seeing a friendly face.

"Did I hear Sebastian say you were recruited from London? Is this your first visit to Meridia?"

Emma smiled at her. "Not exactly. I was here a few weeks ago to meet with officials, but this is my first extended stay."

"You'll find us quite dull, I'm afraid. None of that snap and crackle of the big city here."

"Oh, I don't know," said a deep, masculine voice.

Emma looked down the table and met the glittering gaze of a darkly handsome man with a narrow face and thin hands.

"I think it might be possible to find a spark of something interesting going on in our little city if one tries hard enough," he said, favoring her with the hint of an oily smile.

"My cousin, Romas," Sebastian murmured to her softly. "Beware."

Her back went up immediately. So he thought he could steer her, did he? She gave Romas a bright smile.

"I'm sure I'll be very happy with a more leisurely pace," she told him. "Anyway, I'm going to have my hands full. I won't have time to sample the nightlife."

People were beginning to murmur. She thought she recognized the tall, emaciated minister of finance and the rather portly prime minister as well as the head of the opposition party, all of whom had been pointed out to her earlier. They didn't look friendly at all. She could hardly blame them—and yet, she couldn't help feeling a bit of resentment at the same time. They could at least be polite.

"Cooks at the table," the duke was muttering to himself, searching for his dropped napkin. "What's to become of us?"

"Not just any cook, Uncle," Sebastian said patiently. "Todd went looking for the best and he came back with Miss Valentine."

He looked up and down the table, including them all. "You see, that's how such things are usually managed in the twenty-first century. You have a top-level job opening, you search for someone special to fill it. You look for outstanding candidates, interview them, test them a little, then make an offer and see if your choice takes the bait."

"What is your point, Sebastian?" Romas asked, his tone deceptively lazy.

"Just this, Cousin. Top jobs should be filled competitively. This hereditary nonsense weakens countries that still cling to it."

Gasps started popping up all over the room as each person began to realize just what Sebastian was implying. But Romas was the only one who had a response.

"Are you saying we should post out the job of King of Meridia and take on all comers?" he asked, incredulous. "That's insane."

"I'm not saying that at all," Sebastian replied. "You take me too literally. I'm merely throwing ideas out for open discussion."

"What?" The duke finally left off muttering

about cooks and rejoined the conversation. "That's plain foolishness, my boy. Open discussion never did anyone any good. It just riles people up."

"People need to be riled up every now and then," his nephew told him.

Emma looked at this man who was soon to be king and, for just a moment, she thought she detected a deep, smoldering emotion in his eyes. Was it anger? Resentment? Or grief? It was gone again before she could make a good guess. But it had been real, and it fascinated her.

"At any rate, Miss Valentine is, by all accounts, a wonderful chef. I know she'll prepare a spread that will be talked about for years."

He glanced at her, then looked back at the others. He didn't speak again for almost thirty seconds, but something about him still held their attention. They waited.

"Not only that," he said finally, his voice calm yet full of meaning, "but, as a food expert, I'm hoping she'll be able to help me figure out who poisoned my father."

Shock flashed around the table, quickly followed by outrage.

"Sebastian!" the duke exclaimed.

"What the hell are you talking about?" Romas demanded, half rising from his chair.

"My dear boy," his aunt Trudy cried, her hands fluttering like little birds. "What are you saying?"

Emma turned to look into his golden eyes. There it was again, just a quick glimpse, as though a curtain had been drawn back to reveal his feelings, then let fall again before those emotions could take control. She saw the pulse throbbing at his temple and knew what this was costing him, no matter how cool and disdainful he seemed. He believed his father had been poisoned. But was it true?

She needed to leave. The prince was manipulating these people and she wanted no part of it—and she certainly didn't want to start empathizing with him.

"Let's not play games," he said, taking a sip of wine and slowly lowering the glass again before he looked about at the others. "I've heard the same rumors you've all heard. Well, we'll know soon enough. The final autopsy report is due the day after tomorrow."

"You're ignoring the fact that the preliminary findings were negative," Romas said icily. "You have no grounds for making such an outrageous accusation."

"I'm making no accusations, Romas. I'm only trying to prepare you all for what may be to come. If the autopsy finds evidence of foul play, I won't rest until the guilty party is found and punished."

Romas said something angrily and Sebastian answered him in kind, and Emma took the opportunity to slip away while no one was paying any attention to her. But she didn't go far, just behind the brocade drapes, before she turned and looked back at the prince.

He was still arguing with his cousin, baiting him, really. The more hot-headed Romas got, the cooler Sebastian seemed—like a man in charge. She had a feeling this was probably a pattern that went back to childhood with those two.

"Remind me to stay away from both of them," she murmured to herself as she hurried back into the kitchen. She had enough on her plate without taking on an ancient cousins' rivalry, much less a blood feud or a castle conspiracy. This was just what everyone had warned her against when she'd been trying to decide whether or not to take this job.

"Don't get caught up in the intrigues between different factions," her older half-brother Max had said. "Picking the wrong side could ruin everything."

She'd brushed aside those warnings at the time, but now she saw how perceptive he'd been.

"Focus, focus," she chanted under her breath, vowing to make sure she didn't get drawn into Sebastian's sphere of influence again. She had to keep her mind on her work. After all, that was what had brought her this far. And she had much further to go.

Emma managed to keep her promise to herself for a good eighteen hours. The morning was full of activity as she met with Todd, the coronation manager, to go over the facilities. How and where the food was presented was very important and she was learning as much as she could, soaking up every detail.

It was mid-afternoon as she was finding her way back from the outdoor fields where the medieval tournaments would be performed, when she made the mistake that landed her once again at the prince's feet.

It was his cousin Romas' fault, actually. She'd started up a ramp that rimmed a large inner courtyard when she caught sight of him coming down the same ramp, only on the other side of the opening. Continuing as they were, they were bound to meet halfway around.

That was something she didn't need. Casting about for an escape, she decided to slip into the hedge that bordered the ramp and wait for him to pass. The brush was thick but she squeezed her way into it.

If she'd stayed there, she might have been all right. But she took another step and the next thing she knew her feet slipped out from under her and she was sliding down a steep slope of grass, right through a gap in another hedge, and when she finally righted herself and got back on her feet she realized she'd somehow landed inside the castle maze.

"Oh, bother," she muttered, brushing grass and dirt off the seat of her pants and looking around for the exit. She had a few scratches on her arms but nothing was really hurt except her dignity. Luckily, no one seemed to have seen her wild ride and she had to chuckle when she thought of how she must have looked sliding down the slope.

Oh, well. At least she'd kept her mouth shut— no screams of anguish to bring people running. And she'd managed to avoid Romas. Now to find her way to the exit.

She started in the logical direction, forgetting that logic would work against her in a maze. By the time she realized what she was doing wasn't working, it was too late to just tunnel back through the thick plantings. She'd wound her way deeper into the network and the hedges were now impenetrable and braced by iron fencing.

She was stuck in a maze. This was just plain silly. How could this have happened so fast? Turning this way, then that, she was only getting deeper into trouble. What if she had to start yelling for help? How silly would *that* be?

An old familiar feeling of dread began to tug at her heart, the feeling she'd always had as a child when she'd known her father was going to find out about her latest mistakes. Gritting her teeth, she pushed the feelings away. She'd spent a lifetime learning how to fight off those fears and she wasn't going to give in to them now.

A couple of deep breaths, a quick reminder to herself of how much she'd achieved in her life, and she was all right again. She would get out of this maze and get back to work. It was only a matter of time. After all, these corridors couldn't go on for ever without getting her to something recognizable. Could they?

Still, where was everybody? Maybe the maze was closed. Maybe no one ever came here.

She started off again, walking quickly and wondering which way to go. The faster she went, the more lost she got. And the thirstier. Pictures of desert travelers crawling toward dry water holes began to flit through her mind's eye. She was beginning to imagine her bones as they might be found years later.

"Ah, yes, that chef we hired for the coronation. Looks like she died of starvation, poor thing. You'd think she could have known enough to gnaw on the plant bark at least."

She was still brooding on that tragic scene when she turned a corner, and suddenly found herself face to face with Prince Sebastian.

"Oh!"

She came to a screeching halt and tried to catch her breath. It was lovely to find another human being in the maze—but did it have to be the prince?

CHAPTER FIVE

NEVER mind. Running into the prince was better than constantly running. Emma quickly decided she would pretend she wasn't really lost. Hopefully, he would never guess how close to panic she'd been just a few minutes ago.

Sebastian was dressed in a simple blue shirt and form-fitting jeans and he could have been any handsome young man his age, anywhere. Except—no. She might as well admit it. There was something special about him, something that set him apart. And it wasn't just the fact that she found him incredibly attractive with the afternoon sunlight lighting his hair.

She was glad she'd put on nice slacks and a crisp white shirt, though the dirt and grass stains on the seat of her pants were bound to embarrass her eventually. Her hair was loose, a tangled mess of curls now that she'd had her tussle with the bushes, and she wished she could run a brush through it. Too late.

"Ah, Miss Valentine," he said, one dark eyebrow raised in surprise as he did a double take. "How did you get in here?"

"I just sort of…dropped in." She took a step backwards, then stopped. Where, after all, could she go?

His sharp eyes did not look friendly.

"Didn't you know this maze is forbidden to anyone outside the royal family?" he asked icily.

"Oh. Sorry. I took a wrong turn and lost my footing and found myself crashing through the bushes and…"

Her voice trailed off. Here she was, on the verge of admitting everything. What was it about him that drew these things out of her?

The shoulders. It had to be the shoulders. They were very wide and some primeval instinct in her found comfort in that—as though he were a protective force she could cling to.

If she were the clinging type—something she'd vowed long ago never to be. Still, if she wasn't careful, she might just find herself spilling the details of every humiliating thing she could dredge up to tell him. She started to turn.

"Well, I'll just get out of your way and—"

Stepping forward, he took hold of her arm and frowned at the small scratches. "Crashing through the bushes seems to be dangerous work. Think you can find your way back on your own without destroying the landscaping?"

There was an exclamation from behind him and, for the first time, she realized his aunt Trudy was sitting on a bench a few yards away.

"Don't listen to him, my dear," she chirped. "We're very glad to see you again. Please, come and sit down by my side."

"Oh." Pulling away from the prince, she took a few steps in that direction. She couldn't help but return the older woman's warm smile. "I don't want to intrude."

"You're not intruding at all." She patted the stone seat beside her. "Sit down. We'll have a nice chat."

Sebastian's frown darkened. "She must have something more important to do, Aunt. She looks busy to me."

"How can she be busy? She's wandering about on the grounds. In the maze, no less!" Trudy made room and smiled, offering up a bottle of water, which Emma took gratefully. "You look like you've been through quite an ordeal, my dear. You must rest before you go back. It's so pleasant here."

Trudy was prattling on but Emma suddenly lost all ability to hear. Her gaze had met Sebastian's and though his look was half-exasperated, half-amused, it was also completely aware, as though he knew everything she was thinking and wasn't in the mood to put up with it for much longer. But more than that, his golden eyes cast a spell, drawing her in, and for just a moment the world faded away around them and she could have sworn he'd touched her.

That was impossible, of course. He wasn't even in arm's reach. But she felt as though he'd reached out and run his fingertips down from her cheek to her collarbone, lighting her nerves on fire. She drew her breath in sharply and put her hand to her collarbone, as if to push his away. But there was nothing there.

It seemed like magic.

She blinked, finally, willing herself to look away and begin breathing normally again. And when she glanced back at him, he was looking off into the distance as though nothing had happened at all. Maybe for him it hadn't. And maybe she'd been imagining things.

But she wasn't imagining the feeling of tension in the air and suddenly she realized she'd interrupted an argument of some kind, and that Trudy was glad to have her here. Perhaps she thought Emma would keep Sebastian's anger at bay. Good luck! She was more likely to spark it again.

Looking down at a stack of newspapers on the ground in front of the bench, she began to get an idea of what the discussion had been about. Each one featured a front page article on Sebastian, and each one contained plenty of photos of the prince with beautiful women. Noticing her interest, Trudy began to use her foot to push the papers under the bench, but not before Emma had taken in the tone of the coverage. It seemed uniformly sarcastic and critical.

"Trying to hide my past, Aunt?" he said wryly. "Don't bother. When you make the front page of every local paper, the secrets are out." He pulled a paper out and stared at the cruel headline. "This is what the country I'm to rule thinks of me."

"It doesn't matter," Trudy said soothingly. "Once they get to know you again…"

His bitter smile held not a hint of humor. "My aunt is under the benign illusion that to know me is to love me," he quipped. "*Au contraire*, dear relative. The local governing element knew me well years ago, and none of them could stand me. They loved Julius. They want Julius."

Emma felt a twinge of compassion for the

prince, and suddenly she heard herself blurting out, "Well, Julius didn't love them enough to stick around for them, did he?"

He looked at her as though she'd said something surprising. His mouth suddenly stretched into a lopsided grin with none of his usual irony.

"Out of the mouths of babes," he muttered softly.

"Hey, I'm not a babe," she protested, hoping he didn't suspect her pleasure at seeing a real smile from him.

"Oh, yeah?" He grinned at her. "Could have fooled me. I'll bet you clean up pretty good."

"Sebastian!" Trudy admonished. "None of that."

He shrugged, but his gaze lingered on Emma and she felt a flush of warmth spreading through her system like a shot of brandy on a cold winter day.

"Never mind about the attitude of the town," Trudy said quickly, looking uncomfortable. "Once you're married the attitude will change. Now if only you could manage to find someone suitable."

The corners of Sebastian's wide mouth twitched. "I resent that, Aunt. The women I've dated have been perfectly suitable—for me."

"Suitable as playmates, perhaps."

The look that flashed between the two of them made Emma think they were about to start up their argument again. But before that could happen, Sebastian's expression changed as though something new had occurred to him.

"Speaking of playmates, what happened to Julius' dog?"

Trudy shrugged. "Lago? I'm sure I don't know."

Sebastian frowned thoughtfully. "He wouldn't have taken that mutt with him."

"Perhaps he's down in the stables."

"The stables! He's a house dog." Sebastian seemed outraged at the thought. "I'd better go down and see if I can find him."

"Not yet," Trudy said sharply. "We're still waiting for Agatha."

Emma wondered fleetingly who Agatha was, but the talk about the dog had stirred a memory of her own.

"I had a dog when I was a girl," she murmured, then was surprised to realize she'd said it out loud. The other two were looking at her, so she went on quickly, wrapping it up. "She was my best friend when I was about eight, but I had to get rid of her when we moved into a flat in London."

Her voice made a tiny break over the word "moved" and the pain she'd felt in giving up Heidi swept over her again, made more poignant with passing time. She caught her breath and then her gaze met Sebastian's and, for just a moment, she thought he was going to smile at her again. There was a warmth in his eyes she'd never seen there before. But it disappeared quickly as Trudy started up again.

"Never mind the dog. It's a bride you need."

He nodded, and his look went back to being cynical and a bit world-weary. "I understand. You want to make sure I don't provide any further embarrassment to the family."

"It's not just the family, my dear. It's the country. Think of Meridia."

A rebellious flame flared up in his eyes, but it faded quickly. Emma felt a stirring of sympathy for him. He really seemed to feel trapped by this situation. She wasn't sure she would have liked it any better than he did to be told what you were going to be doing with the rest of your life, no opinions from you allowed.

"With this inflammatory press coverage, finding a bride may be a problem," he said lightly.

Trudy waved that point away with a scoffing sound. "There will be plenty of women who would jump at the chance of marrying the King of Meridia."

"Yes," Sebastian admitted in an offhand manner, "but the kind of woman who would jump at the chance isn't likely to be the kind of woman I'm going to ask, now, is she?"

Trudy's mouth was set, her lips pursed. It was evident she felt she was dealing with a recalcitrant youth who needed to wise up. "You don't have much choice, do you?"

His gaze drifted toward her companion on the bench. "Maybe I should marry Emma," he said, his tone carrying a hint of mockery as he studied her.

He certainly had a knack for bringing the contrarian out in her. That mocking tone really stung.

"I'm sorry, but Emma wouldn't marry you if you were the last man on earth," she said sharply.

He gave a helpless shrug that was all show, an obvious demand for compassion. "You see? Rejected already." His handsome face was a study in tragedy.

"Oh…I didn't really mean it," she said quickly, wishing she could call back the words. "That just wasn't true. I mean…"

He half laughed, his eyes full of amusement. "Of course it wasn't true. Why should it be true? Women never tell the truth."

Emma gasped, truly and honestly shocked at the casual assumption he was making. "What?"

"Don't tell me this is news to you."

For some reason, this attitude made her absolutely furious with him. "You…you're impossible!" she cried, jumping up and taking a step backward as though she was about to make a run for it.

"Exactly what *I'm* afraid of," Trudy muttered, rising from her seat. "I think we need Agatha." She frowned at Sebastian, seemingly genuinely annoyed with him at last. "She knows how to keep you in line. Wait here." And she hurried off.

Emma watched her go, wondering again who this Agatha might be—and marking the direction Trudy took, keeping it in mind for her own departure.

"Sit down," Sebastian said, dropping down himself and taking her hand to pull her into the seat beside him. "She'll be back in a few minutes."

She settled beside him, staying on the edge of the seat as though ready to jump up and run at the slightest chance. She didn't know why she wasn't following Trudy out and leaving herself. Instead, she was sitting beside this large handsome man who infuriated her and then made her pulse flutter just by looking at her. Was she crazy?

There was a short answer to that question: yes!
She began to gather herself.

"Well, I'd better go too."

He captured her hand and held it in his.

"I wish you'd stay," he said. "For my aunt's
sake. She'll be more comfortable. You saw how
anxious she was to have you join us." His wide
mouth twitched at the corners. He looked down
at the way her hand looked in his and a faint
frown formed as he released her. "I think she
doesn't want to be alone with me."

"Why on earth not?" she said, astonished.

He shrugged and looked away, rubbing his
neck with one hand. "She's afraid of what I'll ask
her."

That stopped her in her tracks. She thought
back to the night before when he'd brought up the
suspicions of poisoning in his father's death. Had
he been serious? She wasn't sure. Something
about the way he'd used it as a weapon against his
cousin—and maybe against other targets she
wasn't aware of—made her think he was manipulating things with motives she couldn't understand.

Later, alone in her room, she'd thought over
what had happened and decided it was almost as
though he'd been trying to flush someone out and

uncover some secrets. She wished she knew more of the background so that she could make her own judgements. She'd even called her cousin Louise back in London and asked her to help.

"I've got no Internet access here," Emma had told her. "And no way to get to a public library. Do you think you could do a little research for me?"

"Sure, I'll do what I can and call you back," her willing cousin had said.

"Great. I feel like I'm walking on eggshells. I need a map of the territory."

"Okey dokey. I'll get back to you as soon as I can." Louise's bright voice always lightened her spirits. "In the meantime, watch out for land mines."

The prince was probably the biggest land mine she knew, and here she was sitting with him again. She'd never been known as a risk taker before. What the heck was she doing here?

"Your aunt seems to be in a big hurry to get you married," she noted, not eager to stay with the subject of why Trudy might not want to answer Sebastian's questions.

"Naturally. They all are. They're terrified of leaving open the opportunity for another scandal."

"Scandal?" She wasn't sure what he was referring to.

He gave her a quizzical look. "Surely you know about my brother."

She frowned. She knew she'd heard something about why he'd abdicated, but she couldn't quite remember the details.

"What was the story on your brother? Wasn't it something like the Duke of Windsor and Mrs Simpson?"

Sebastian's slight smile was cold. "There are similarities, but it's not quite the same. In that case, the King of England gave up the throne because he was in love with a divorced woman. These days we don't care all that much about divorced women. My brother's case was a little different. His paramour wasn't divorced, but he *was* male."

"Oh. And we still have a bit of a problem with that, do we?"

"Here in Meridia we do."

"So who was scandalized?"

"The entire country went nuts," he said. "There were riots in the streets."

"You're kidding." She was truly surprised. "I would have thought most people could take things like that in their stride these days."

"Not a chance. Meridia is an old-fashioned place with traditional values. The twenty-first century is pretty much still just a rumor around here. Meridians don't like it when one of their own does something they consider out of bounds."

"I see." She also saw that such narrow expectations might be a problem for a man like Sebastian who was used to a wider worldview.

"Everyone had pinned hopes on Julius." His eyes narrowed as he looked off into the sky. "He excelled at everything all through school, academically and athletically. He was the golden-haired child, sure to be a great leader once he became king. Everyone said so. He was going to lead the country into some sort of new Promised Land of milk and honey."

He paused, slowly shaking his head. "And then his time came, and he turned his back on the whole thing. I couldn't believe it when my uncle called to tell me what had happened. Everyone was stunned. He'd never done anything to indicate he might throw it all away. To the contrary. He was such a team player. The people were looking forward to having him as their ruler. And now…"

He turned to look at her, searching her eyes as though she might have an answer to the mystery.

And she stared back, wishing she had what he was looking for. From offhand things he'd said, she assumed he wasn't the most enthusiastic heir to the throne the country had ever seen.

"Well, now they have you," she said, hoping to sound perky and supportive. "Despite those terrible headlines, I'm sure they're thrilled."

"With me?" He looked astonished, then laughed aloud. "Oh, Emma. If you only knew."

"What?"

He gazed at her for a moment, then looked away. "I was the black sheep of the family. Every time Julius did something good, I did something bad."

He grimaced. "And now the good people of Meridia are stuck with the loser and they're very worried. If the perfect prince could run off the rails like that, what will the royal rebel do?"

She bit her lip. He was trying to sound a note of cynical bravado, but she thought she could sense a thread of deep bitterness behind it.

"Are you really such a black sheep?" she asked softly.

He looked at her again, hesitated, then gave her a humorless smile.

"I was. It was a point of pride with me. And it put me at constant odds with my father."

She laughed softly. "That's not so special. I know something about fathers."

"Ah, you have one too, do you?"

"Yes, I do." Her smile faded as she thought of him.

"My father must have disowned me a hundred times over the years," he added.

"But he always took you back."

"Yes." The bitterness had crept into his smile. "My mother made him."

"Oh." She knew his mother had died about two years before. "Were you close to her?"

He looked surprised at her question, but he answered with simple honesty. "Yes. Very."

The emotion in his voice touched a deep chord in her and she frowned. She didn't want to be touched by him. Instinctively, she knew how dangerous that could be.

Suddenly she was completely aware of him, aware of his smooth, tanned skin, his long, tapered fingers, aware of the way his muscular thighs pulled the material of his jeans taut, aware of his body heat.

"I should go," she said, though she couldn't seem to get her muscles to help her achieve that goal.

"You're a big believer in responsibility, aren't

you?" he said casually, turning toward her and resting his arm on the seat behind her so that he was so close, his face was almost touching hers. "Do you ever break the rules, Emma?"

He was looking at her in that mesmerizing way again and she was breathless.

"Rules?" she said, very much afraid that her voice had squeaked on the word. "What rules?"

He smiled. "That's the ticket," he said, his voice a low rumble. "Forget the rules. Follow your heart."

"I…" She cleared her throat. "I prefer to follow my head," she said, hoping he couldn't tell that her voice was shaking.

For some reason, he'd taken her chin in his large hand and was looking down at her.

"You have very kissable lips, Emma Valentine," he noted softly, as though it were news she could use.

"No."

She wasn't sure if she was rejecting his opinion on her lips or just generally telling him to stop, because that head she'd thought she could count on was spinning like a top and thinking straight was getting to be a monumental chore.

"Yes, you do," he countered, his long fingers stroking her cheek. "I think we should try it out."

She blinked. "Try what out?"

One dark eyebrow raised. "Kissing."

"Oh."

She couldn't think of an argument against it. Her mind was fuzzy, though, so it wasn't really fair to test her like this. She tried to think, but feeling was crowding that out. His fingers felt like heaven on her face, conjuring up pure excitement.

He wanted to kiss her. And suddenly she'd never wanted anything more than she wanted that kiss to happen. She lifted her lips, hungry to taste his. Her eyes were closing and she was leaning his way, ready.

But he hesitated a beat longer than she expected. In a flash, she knew why. He was listening to see if his aunt was coming back yet. Somehow, that thought was like cold water. It woke her up and she jerked away.

"Wait a minute," she said, eyes wide open now. "Hold everything. This is ridiculous." Putting both hands on his chest, she pushed him back. He looked puzzled and bemused by her reaction.

"Against kissing, are you?"

"I didn't come here for kissing."

"What did you come here for, then?"

"Cooking, of course."

His smile was rueful. "That's right. I forgot—

the chef thing." He lightly stroked her cheek again, but this time the sultry, sexy, languorous element was missing from his touch. "Are you a chef twenty-four hours a day?"

"I try to be," she said stoutly, pushing his hand away. "Aren't you a prince twenty-four hours a day?"

He groaned. "I try *not* to be."

"Yoo hoo."

A female voice calling from somewhere in the maze startled them both. Sebastian sat up straight, then rose from the bench.

"Never mind," he said, effectively dismissing Emma. "You don't have to wait. Here's Agatha. You can go." He gave her a quick smile. "Released from your bonds."

"Oh."

She was relieved. At least she thought she was. Rising as well, she looked from one path to the other. "But what way do I go?"

He pointed out the route Trudy had taken. "The secret to the maze is a formula. Left, left, right. The pattern repeats over and over. Once you get it, you never forget it."

That seemed simple enough.

"Well, goodbye." She looked back at him, but he was already turning away.

"Goodbye," he said over his shoulder, going in the opposite direction. "Thanks for your help."

She took a few steps and glanced back. A beautiful auburn-haired woman in a long, gauzy dress who had come in from the other side was launching herself into Sebastian's arms.

Turning back quickly, Emma hurried off, but not before she heard snatches of their greeting.

"Hello, darling," Sebastian was saying. "I've missed you. It's been too long."

"Who's that?" the young woman asked, obviously noticing Emma's retreating form.

"What? Oh, nobody..."

Nobody.

Emma felt, for just a moment, as though she'd been stabbed in the heart.

CHAPTER SIX

NOBODY!

Well, it served Emma right for letting herself think, even for a fleeting moment, that a man like Sebastian might be interested in her. He was a prince, for heaven's sake! Everyone knew what they were like. Even his aunt understood his ways and was trying to reform him in order to be presentable to a decent young woman. There was nothing to be gained in throwing your heart over the moon.

Nobody!

She had a quick flashback to the nights her own mother had stalked around the flat in a robe, waiting hours for the phone to ring, her eyes red and swollen. Emma had vowed at a very young age that she would never let a man put her in that position—that she would never, ever yearn after a man who didn't really want her. And so far, she'd kept her word. This was no time to risk breaking her promise.

Yet, here she was, hobnobbing with royalty and tempting fate. Idiot that she'd proved to be.

Nobody!

Adrenaline surged every time she replayed that word in her head. But she was out of the maze. Left, left, right had worked.

And she was a wiser woman as well—and not one to fall for the sweet sham seduction of princes. So there.

Nobody. Hah. The man didn't know what he was talking about.

Emma was on the phone with her cousin Louise later that evening when someone tapped on her door. Her heart jumped and she had a few seconds of anticipation before she realized what she was doing and quickly reined it in.

"Someone's at my door," she told her cousin.

"Better answer it," Louise teased. "It might be the prince."

Close as she was to her cousin, she hadn't told her about the maze encounter. She was still too embarrassed knowing how easily she'd fallen into a swoon over the man. Louise didn't know much beyond the original assault with the water-polo ball. But she did know Emma was interested in the background of the royal family. It had been the results of her research that she'd called to tell about.

Emma had finally located the castle library earlier that day. There were acres of books on Meridian history and she'd brought a stack of them back to her room. But when she'd tried to find newspaper articles about the death of the king, she hadn't come across anything beyond the barest basic details. She'd found plenty of coverage of the king's lingering illness and death, but no mention of poison, or even of suspicions. Still, there was something curious. A few days after the death and after the funeral, a few papers appeared to have had articles cut out and removed. Luckily, Louise had been able to fill in some of the gaps for her.

"None of the articles I found actually came right out and said poison was suspected," she'd just been telling Emma. "They hinted around a lot, though. 'Foul play' not ruled out and such. And one article right after the funeral did mention an autopsy."

So Sebastian's charges weren't totally without foundation. Which brought up new questions, of course, such as—who might have wanted the king to die?

Emma still had the phone with her as she

opened the door and found Will Harris standing there.

"Oh, hello," she said, thrown off guard. "It's Dr Will," she said mindlessly into the phone.

"Good evening, Emma," he said in his low, masculine voice as she invited him in. "The prince sent me to check on your wounds from this afternoon in the maze."

"Oh."

Emma was speechless, but Louise, who had heard every word, wasn't.

"Oh, my God, the prince sent a doctor to check on you? Emma! I knew it. I knew we'd get a fairy-tale romance out of this. Oh, I wish I had time to fly over and see this for myself."

"Louise, I'll have to call you back," she said, clicking off in hopes of keeping her cousin's enthusiasm away from Will's ears. She smiled at the man. "That's so nice of you…and of the prince, of course. But it's nothing. Just scratches. See?"

He saw, but he'd brought along antibiotic cream and bandages and he was determined to use them. He worked on her injuries for a good half an hour and they chatted pleasantly all the while.

"You want to take care of things like this, even common scratches," he told her. "A little extra effort can avoid scars."

That reminded her of the ugly wound she'd seen on Sebastian's side the day before when he'd wrestled with Will on the pool deck. Though she knew it was none of her business, hesitantly, she asked Will about it.

He didn't answer right away and she was afraid she'd offended him.

"The prince was stabbed defending Agatha's honor," he said softly at last, his eyes suddenly burning with a harsh light. "He foiled a kidnapping attempt. And that's all I can tell you, as he doesn't want the incident talked about."

"I see."

Well, she didn't really see. Because this was about Agatha again. Will spoke her name as though he assumed she knew the woman, not realizing it was a name she was learning to despise. But all the same, her heart was thumping with the thought of Sebastian doing something noble, as she was sure he had. It was hard to hate him, no matter how much she tried.

She liked Will a lot. His calm good nature was a soothing antidote. At times she thought she caught hints of a secret sorrow in his manner, but he never failed to say something kind and clever.

And he was very good-looking. Still, after he left and she shut the door and leaned against it, she couldn't help but notice that he didn't make her blood zing the way the prince did. Not at all.

It warmed her heart a little—just a bit—to think Sebastian had remembered her scratches and sent help. But then, he would have done as much for anyone, she was sure.

"And remember," she whispered to herself, like someone who couldn't keep from touching a sore spot, "to him, you're nobody."

But that didn't matter, because she was going to give him the best coronation dinner that had ever been spread out before a king. It was going to be a point of pride with her to make him eat his words.

The coronation was only a little over two weeks away and she knew that every day was going to be more and more precious to her as they dwindled down. She was going to do a good job. She had no doubt about that. But so much could go wrong that was out of her control.

Tomorrow, Todd was taking her down to the town market so that she could check out the local produce and incorporate as much of it as possible into the menus. She would have to order ahead of time and have supplies trucked up to the castle and she was looking forward to seeing what was avail-able. Plus, a day away from the castle would be a good thing. Hopefully, she could find ways to avoid the prince for now—and maybe even for ever.

Sebastian's eyes were glazing over. He was walking down a corridor in the castle with two of the most boring men he knew, his uncle the duke, and the Earl of Grogna, Minister of Accounts. The two of them were talking such rot he couldn't keep his mind on what they were saying. What was the point of arguing the details of Meridian monetary policy when he wasn't sure he was going to be in Meridia in another week or two?

He began to hang back a bit, planning his escape. The other two men were engrossed in their argument and might not even notice if he slipped away. They were just passing the library when something caught his eye.

He stopped. The two men went on, just as he'd hoped. And he walked softly into the library toward where Emma was trying to reach a book set on a shelf high above her. She'd pulled a small stepstool over and climbed upon it. Now she was on tiptoe, stretching her arm as high as she could and just barely touching the target with her fingertips.

He grinned. Nothing made his day more than helping damsels in distress. Especially damsels with such nicely rounded backsides, set off to perfection by her soft velour pants.

She hadn't heard him approach, so she started when he came up behind her.

"Oh!"

"Allow me," he murmured, reaching over her and taking the book from the shelf. But he didn't bring it down right away. The reach had brought his body up against hers and she felt very good there. A fresh, spicy scent seemed to be emanating from her thick hair, and that, along with her softness, brought on a sense of sweet seduction that filled him like a drug. Closing his eyes to savor it, he turned into the hollow of her neck and pressed his face against her skin.

She gasped, but she didn't pull away, and suddenly he wanted her with a deep, throbbing ache that surprised him. He touched the lobe of her delicate ear with the tip of his tongue for just a scattering of seconds, then gave a sigh that came directly from this new and very intense longing.

He knew it was time to draw back. He could hear the duke and the accounts minister returning and calling for him. Besides, the evidence of his desire for her was becoming all too clear and he knew she had to feel it. He had to go. But she felt so good, it was very hard to make himself do it.

"Sorry," he whispered to her, handing her the book. "So sorry, Emma."

He knew she wouldn't know if he was apologizing for the erotic intrusion, or for the fact that he couldn't take it further. And truth be told, he wasn't sure which he meant either. But he did enjoy the completely stunned look in her eyes. He touched her cheek gently, then turned to rejoin his companions. But the feel of her body and the look in her eyes stayed with him for a long time.

Things in Emma's life never seemed to go according to plan and the luck she'd once had seemed to have deserted her ever since she'd arrived in this strange little country. Todd had a last-minute emergency and couldn't take her into town, but he'd given her instructions on how to get there and what to do once she arrived. She'd taken a castle car and headed out on her own in a drizzling rain.

It wasn't long before trouble erupted. Swerving to miss a careening motorcyclist, she ended up in a ditch that was rapidly filling with mud and her wheels spun uselessly when she tried to drive back out.

So there she was in the rain, shoving rocks and pieces of stray wood under the back wheels of the car, trying to build a platform for traction, when she heard another car coming down the road from the castle. She didn't even look up. The way her luck had been running lately, she just had a feeling she knew who this was going to be.

The car slowed to a stop and she heard a window being rolled down.

"Emma, what happened?"

She closed her eyes and sighed. Yes. It was him. Why? Why?

"Need some help?"

Swinging around, she glared at Sebastian, fully aware of how she must look in the silly yellow anorak she'd found in the trunk of the car, with her wet hair plastered to her face.

"No, thank you," she said crisply, determined that he understand that she wasn't in awe of him, despite how she'd fallen into a swoon over him the night before in the library. "I can take care of this myself."

"Emma, don't be ridiculous. I'm going to call the castle. They'll send someone out to handle it."

He flipped open his phone and began to punch in a number.

She knew that was probably sensible, but she resented it none the less. "Then I won't have a car," she countered.

His smile was wide and innocent. "You'll have me."

"You!"

She put all the pent-up anger she had into the word and aimed it at him like a missile. He was startled.

"Hey, I'm not so bad."

She wasted one more good glare on him, then turned back to her work. She could hear him telling someone to come out and get the car, but that only made her work harder and faster. If she could just get a good piece of wood under the tire, she might have a chance to move this wreck and get back on the road before they came.

"Come on, Emma. Get in the car."

"No, thank you," she called back, waving a hand at him. "Just move along. There's nothing to see here."

"Emma." He was sounding impatient now. "If you don't get into this car in the next five seconds I'm going to get out and pick you up and…"

But he didn't wait five seconds. Before she had

time to react, he was already out of the car and coming toward her and then his hands were on her shoulders and he was staring right down into her wet face.

"Emma, tell me why you're so angry. What have I done?"

She gasped. He was so sure of himself—and so straightforward. He didn't give her time to mount her defenses.

"Nothing," she said, avoiding his intense gaze.

"Right. This feels like the old 'if you don't know by now, I'm not going to tell you' ploy to me."

She tried to twist out of his grasp. "It's nothing. Really."

"Was it yesterday? In the maze? Or what happened in the library? Or something I've done since?"

She looked up and that was her big mistake. Once she'd been captured by his gaze, she couldn't seem to break free of it.

"I…well…can't you just leave me alone?"

"No. I can't. Tell me."

She drew in a deep, shuddering breath. "All right. If you really want to know."

She hesitated. How was she going to approach this? Could she be as direct as he was?

"Who was that woman who came into the maze as I was leaving?" she heard herself saying, as though a truth serum had been poured down her throat. She hadn't meant to say it. She knew it made her look jealous to say it. And yet, there it was. She'd said it.

"My aunt Trudy?" He made a face, then realized who she meant. "Oh, do you mean Agatha? Emma, Agatha is my sister."

"Oh."

His sister.

Relief swelled in her like a small internal hurricane. She hadn't even known he had a sister.

The humiliation of it all! To think that finding out the woman was just his sister could make her weak with happiness. She had to turn her head away so he wouldn't see it in her eyes.

"Why would that bother you?" he insisted, looking truly puzzled.

She swallowed hard. He wasn't going to let it go, was he? Well, then, she would just have to be honest. She'd gone this far.

"It isn't that, really," she said, only half lying. "It was what you said when she asked who I was."

She glanced back at his face. He was obviously completely at sea.

"You'll have to remind me. What did I say?"

"You said…" She swallowed hard again. This was more difficult than she'd thought it would be. "You said I was nobody."

There. It was out. Now he knew how terribly insecure she really was. What a ninny—she couldn't even laugh off something like that and go on with her life. She'd been obsessing about it for hours. And now he knew.

His face twisted in denial and he shook his head. "I couldn't have said that. I wouldn't have said that. It's not true."

Okay, time to show a little courage, at least. Taking a deep breath, she forced herself to look up into his eyes again.

"I know it's not true," she said stoutly. "But I heard it loud and clear."

He thought for a moment, frowning intently as he went back over the previous day, and suddenly his face cleared.

"Oh, I know what happened," he said at last. "Agatha said, 'Who's that?' as you were walking away and I said, 'Nobody you would know.' That's all. I knew the two of you hadn't met. Agatha just arrived from Spain." His expression changed. Reaching out, he pulled her closer again.

"Emma, I'm sorry if you thought…"

No, she was the sorry one—sorry that she'd ever brought it up. Her face was flaming now. She believed his explanation. It fitted. And she *wanted* to believe it. But that hardly mattered any more, because all this was so tangled up with her impossible feelings for this man and the kiss that had been so close and then hadn't happened and then the encounter in the library. Deep and disturbing emotions that she'd learned to cover up over the years that were now starting to stir inside her.

And finally, the sudden, strange urge she had to reach up and fold herself into his arms, as though that would somehow protect her from the wet and the cold and from ever being hurt again. She'd never felt anything like it. The hunger for his embrace filled her with such longing, she almost whimpered aloud. And for just a moment, she thought she saw an answering impulse in his eyes.

But the moment was lost as the castle Jeep came bumbling to a stop beside them and two workmen jumped out, ready to deal with the mired car.

By the time the two of them were in Sebastian's car and headed toward town, she'd regained control and recaptured her sanity.

"You can just drop me at the market," she said,

sitting stiffly on her side of the car. "I'm sure you have places to go, people to see."

"Oh, yes. My life is a mad whirl of activity." He glanced at her as he slowed to let another car pass. "To tell the truth, I'm running away from home."

"What are you talking about?"

He sighed. "It wasn't bad enough that I had to sit through a two-hour lecture on Meridian foreign policy from my uncle, a man who couldn't find Latvia on a map if his life depended on it. I also had to stand up again and again for a flock of tailors who kept interrupting in order to take my measurements for every ceremonial uniform this country ever authorized. Then the secretary of the council called to say they wanted to see me for a discussion of my attitude problem." He shook his head. "It was too much. I had to get out of there. I couldn't take any more."

She was frowning, caught up in his problems in spite of herself. "You don't already have all those uniforms?"

"Sure I do, but I need new ones. I'm bigger in the shoulders these days."

She glanced at his wide and very attractive shoulders. She couldn't help it. And then she flushed again when he caught her at it.

This was getting repetitive. She turned her head and looked out the window at the countryside. The rain had stopped and the sun was breaking through the clouds, pouring golden light over the green landscape. Everything seemed fresh and new.

Landlocked and hidden in the mountains, tucked between Italy, Switzerland and Austria, Meridia had managed to avoid most of the wars and cultural dislocations of the twentieth century. But that also meant the country sometimes seemed left behind by history and the technological revolution. Still, that only gave it a certain unique charm.

The capital town of Chadae was just ahead. She could see small, brightly colored houses spilling over the hillside like a child's set of blocks. Sebastian pulled off onto a turnout and switched off the engine. She turned to him in surprise.

"What are you doing?"

He gave her a wink, leaned over and pulled open the glove compartment in front of her, taking out two pairs of dark glasses.

"Here's a lesson," he said. "If you're going to hang out with royalty, learn to go incognito." He handed her one pair of sunglasses and put the other on himself.

She gave him a scathing glance. *"That's* supposed to be incognito?" They hid his beautiful eyes, but everything else about him still screamed, "Royalty here!"

He shrugged. "I usually do a better job. I didn't prepare myself sufficiently. I'm going to have to get back into the swing of these things."

"Never mind," she said, passing the glasses back to him. "I'm not really planning to do much hanging with royalty."

"You're hanging with me today."

"No, I'm not."

"What do you call this?"

She was speechless for a moment. He was making bad assumptions. "I'm accepting a ride into town. And I shouldn't even be doing that."

"Why the hell not?"

He couldn't be this clueless. "Come on, Sebastian, don't pretend to be dense. You're the prince. I'm the chef. The prince and the hired help don't go gallivanting around together. It isn't done. And I'm not going to do it." She folded her arms and stared straight ahead.

"You know what they say about the best laid plans of mice and men." He waited for a response, then frowned when she refused to give him one. "So you're saying you don't want to be seen with me? What a snob you are, Emma Valentine."

She sighed, looking heavenward. "Okay. I'm a snob. My standards are high. I refuse to be seen with princes."

He looked into the rearview mirror and adjusted the glasses. "Do I look like a real prince to you?" he asked doubtfully, looking hard at his reflection.

"Yes." She was adamant.

He made a face. "Okay. And you look like a princess."

She wrinkled her nose with disdain. "I do not."

"You could." He actually looked hopeful.

"But I don't."

Looking at her, he started to laugh.

"Well, I have to admit, right now you look a lot more like a drowned cat. A very bad-tempered drowned cat."

She was trying hard not to smile, but it was getting almost impossible to keep a straight face around him. The harder she tried to dislike him, the more he turned on the charm, just to prove he could. She was fighting a losing battle here and she knew it.

"You may try to avoid royalty, Emma, but I'm afraid royalty is going to come your way, regardless. At least for the time being." He handed the glasses back again. "So in the future you might want to be prepared with extra pairs of dark glasses and a good trench coat at all times. Just in case."

He was saying these things with a good-natured earnestness that made her want to laugh. Biting her lip, she put the dark glasses on and looked at him. He grinned.

"And exactly who am I supposedly hiding from?" she asked.

"The media." There was no hint of humor in his voice now. A quiet bitterness had taken its place. "They're like leeches. Once they get you in their sights, you're done for. They can make life hell on earth if you let them."

She stared at him, wondering if a few little sarcastic articles were all that had happened to make him so hostile to the press. But before she could ask, he started up the engine and pulled back out onto the highway.

"Listen, would you like to see some of Meridian life?"

"Why, yes, but—"

"Come on. We'll swing by the markets and you can get a flavor of what's available. Then I'll introduce you to my old nanny."

"Your nanny lives here in town?"

"Yes. She didn't want to stay at the castle any more than I did."

"It…sounds like fun."

She was smiling, but, deep down, she knew she was crazy to let him sweep her away like this. She was surely going to regret it.

The two of them wandered through the outdoor markets in their dark glasses. It was a little too warm for trench coats once the clouds disappeared over the horizon and the sun took over. No one paid any attention to either one of them as they made their way through the crowds. There were children playing hoop games and boys kicking a soccer ball back and forth and dogs waiting patiently for bits of scrap food to be thrown their way and babies in carriages and sellers shouting out sudden discounts or fabulous new qualities discovered in their wares. Emma was charmed by it all.

"This place has the quality that history reproductions strive for and never quite achieve," she noted. "It's old, unique, colorful and authentic."

Weaving their way between tanks of live lobster and other seafood, they stopped before a huge fish tank filled with large silver-blue fish with faces like bulldogs who swam lazily from one side to the other.

"What is this?" Emma asked, struck by the strangeness.

"This is the unicomus, our national fish," Sebastian told her. "They only live in Lake Chadae and are found nowhere else."

"Impressive," Emma said, thinking from the culinary perspective. Fish was a specialty of hers.

"Come see the truffle display," he said, drawing her away. "We are known for our outstanding truffles. Our one claim to international fame."

"Ooh, truffles!"

She could think of lots of uses for the magnificent specimens he showed her. In fact, the markets were a gold mine of produce of all kinds, making her imagination run wild with ideas for the coronation dinner.

They strolled down toward the lake. A walkway hugged the edge of the water and Sebastian led her out along it, telling her of boyhood adventures as they went. A cluster of young boys playing soccer sent a ball shooting their way and suddenly the prince was an athlete again, using a few slick moves to send the ball back over their heads and right into the goal.

"Bravo!" a few of them cried, applauding the effort.

He took a bow and laughed, returning to Emma

with a look on his face that told her his usual ironic reserve had been obliterated for the time being. But he was rubbing the area where the scar was and she remembered what Will had told her the night before. Now she knew that it was his sister whose honor he'd defended.

"Come on down to the marina," he said, catching her hand in his. "I'll show you where I first learned to sail."

It was only a few steps away. The blue tarps, white sails and colorful flags flying gave the area a festive air. There were people fishing off an old wooden pier, and a group of young men gathering around a number of sailboats docked along the marina. Sebastian knew some of them and went over to speak to them, but Emma stayed behind, leaning on the railing and enjoying the sunlight on the water.

Or trying to enjoy it. She hadn't been there long when a pair of teenagers sidled up next to her and began talking in tones obviously meant for her to hear.

"Yeah, that's Prince Sebastian all right. I'd know him anywhere," said one. "I guess he's going to be king."

"They say he killed his brother to get him out of the way, you know," the other replied, glancing at Emma and then pulling his cap down over his eyes.

Shocked, she had to put in her two cents.

"Prince Julius isn't dead," she told them sternly. "He fell in love with…someone…and abdicated the throne."

"Oh, yeah?" said the first boy. "Have you seen him?"

She hesitated. "Well, no, but…"

The boy shrugged. "No one here has, either."

"But he's alive," she insisted indignantly.

The boy shrugged again. "There's some who won't believe that until they see it with their own eyes," he said as he and his companion began to drift off.

Taking a deep breath, Emma tried to calm herself. They were just silly boys, after all. She shouldn't take what they said seriously. But she was afraid such rumors were only the tip of the iceberg here in Meridia, just a sample of what Sebastian was going to have to deal with.

He was back a moment later, looking happier than ever. "They're training hard and hoping to qualify for the next Olympics," he told her enthusiastically. "I told them I might be able to help with the design of a new hull they're working on. I've got some great ideas."

"You design sailboats?" she asked in surprise.

"Sure. You didn't think I spent all my time on the water working on my tan, did you?"

No, she had never thought that. Partying was a factor that had come to mind. It was a relief to know that wasn't all he'd been living for.

They made their way back to the marketplace. Suddenly, Sebastian seized her hand and leaned close. "I think I've been identified," he murmured, nodding toward where a small group of young women were gathering, looking excited and whispering to one another as they trained their attention on him. "We'll have to make a run for it."

"You lead the way," she said, suppressing a smile.

They started off slowly, weaving in and out of stalls, but, looking back, it was obvious they were being followed. Sebastian made a sudden turn and they found themselves in a dark alley.

"Run," Sebastian urged, holding her hand.

They ran, turning down another alley, and then another, until they were both laughing and gasping for air and Emma found herself in Sebastian's arms.

She pulled away quickly, but not before taking in enough of his long, hard form to memorize it for life. That was going to sustain her on some long, lonely nights.

"Did we lose them?" she said breathlessly.

"I think so." Turning his head, he listened intently. "Yes." Looking back down at her, he smiled.

She smiled back. A warm, thrilling sense of connection sprang between them.

And then it was gone as Sebastian deliberately turned away.

"Let's see," he said in a casual way that let her know he'd sensed the same thing she had and that he was disturbed by it too. "I think it's only a couple of blocks to my old nanny's house. Ready?"

She nodded. He'd turned the day into an adventure she couldn't resist.

CHAPTER SEVEN

SEBASTIAN's nanny was large and loving and ready to claim Emma as her own right from the start. Her name was Tina Marie and she ran a small café in the front section of her house. In the back, she had cookbooks and exotic spices and special kitchen gadgets that could have kept Emma enthralled for days.

Instead, she just got a quick hour to browse through all the treasures while Tina Marie and Sebastian caught up on their news.

"It's been so long since I've seen this one," the effusive woman kept repeating, surging back to give her grown-up charge another kiss on the cheek where he sat at her big kitchen table, drinking the thick, sweet coffee she'd served him. "You're too thin. Here, have a cherry tart. Have another bonbon."

"No, thanks," Sebastian said, pushing the food away. "I'm saving room for lunch."

"You haven't had lunch? I'll fix you some."

"No, no—"

"I know! I'll fix you a picnic basket. You must take your beautiful lady up to the watch meadow and show her the view." She hugged Emma, who was feeling so adored, she didn't even protest about being called beautiful. "Then you can eat your lunch there. It will be wonderful!"

She went through the kitchen like a whirlwind, grabbing supplies, cutting slices of bread into interesting shapes, mixing ingredients, and talking all the while.

At one point, Emma asked her how she came to be Sebastian's nanny.

"I was just a girl when I was hired as Queen Marguerite's private attendant. She was a new bride from Italy—didn't know a word of any other language but her own. And Sebastian's father, the king, though he knew Italian very well, refused to speak it to her. Thought it best to force her into quick immersion into Meridian." She shook her head, her eyes on the distant memories. "She was so lonely, poor thing. Scared to death, so worried that she would make mistakes. Every morning I would find her pillow wet from her tears."

Emma glanced at Sebastian. His face was impassive, his eyes unreadable, but she felt his anger over his mother's misery. Was that at least a partial clue as to why he often seemed to have a simmering bitterness deep in his soul?

She turned back to Tina Marie. "Did you help her?" she asked.

"I did the best I could, but I was a servant. In those days, that made quite a gulf, you know." She sighed. "But I loved her right from the beginning. She was a wonderful lady. So beautiful. She died much too young."

In those days, that made quite a gulf... The words lingered in Emma's mind. Things hadn't changed as much as Tina Marie might think.

She asked about local customs she might want to incorporate into the menu for the coronation and was immediately inundated with cookbooks and lists of secret ingredients.

"You've heard about our truffles, of course. World famous. People come from everywhere to buy them."

"Oh, yes. I already have plans for truffles."

"Then you must include our small sweet breakfast breads, called eirhorns. And our famous eikenberry jam."

"Don't forget cornberry wine," Sebastian interspersed.

"Oh, yes," Tina Marie cried. "The best sweet wine ever. Not made with real cornberries, of course. These days we use eikenberries. Too many people are allergic to the real thing."

"Too bad," Sebastian said. "I hate when traditions go by the board that way. Cornberries make a very potent brew," Sebastian went on, waxing euphoric about the past again. "At its best, it's got a kick like moonshine. When we were teenagers—"

"When you were teenagers, you did a lot of things that would be better left to fade into the mists of time," Tina Marie said sharply.

Sebastian grinned, leaning back in his chair. Watching him, Emma thought she'd never seen him look so relaxed.

"So what do you think about Julius?" he was asking his nanny. "Were you shocked?"

Tina Marie waved a dismissive hand. "Not in the least. You know very well I used to tell you he couldn't hold a candle to you in any way, if you would only make an effort."

"Ah, there's the rub. Is the effort worth the prize?"

Tina Marie came to a standstill for the first time since they'd arrived. She stared at Sebastian for a long, silent moment. Finally, she asked, "Are you going to do it?"

He stared right back and didn't say a word.

"Your coronation is in two weeks."

"Yes, it is."

"Will you be here for it?"

His smile was strangely bittersweet. "Ah, Tina Marie, you know me so well."

"Indeed I do, but the question still stands."

"I don't know," he said quietly.

Drawing in a deep breath, she began to bustle again, packing the provisions away in a picnic basket.

"You know you were meant for the throne," she said. "I used to tell you—"

"That was then, Tina Marie. This is now. Things change."

She glared at him over her shoulder. "Responsibilities stay the same."

"For responsible people. That's something I've worked hard to guard against being."

She shook a spoon at him. "And in doing so, you only proved the opposite."

But she was soon kissing his cheeks again. As they left with their heavy picnic basket in tow she hugged Emma and whispered in her ear, "I can see that you care for him. Please, watch his back. That is where the knives usually find their mark."

* * *

Sebastian leaned back and watched Emma pulling things out of the picnic basket, tasting and exclaiming over one thing after another. He was only half listening. Looking out over the cliff at the lake and the town below, he felt a swelling in his heart that was almost painful.

Despite everything, he loved this place. How could he not? The rivers ran like the blood in his body, its soil was his flesh. He could stay away for years, he could never come back again, and it still would be a part of him—a part of his heart, a part of his life, the core of who he was.

But could he stay here? Could he be a ruler? That was another question, one he hadn't even answered for himself as yet.

Did he want to? That he could answer, and the answer was no. But Tina Marie was right. It was his duty to stay and take care of his country and its people. But it had been Julius' duty before him.

Emma was setting arrangements of the food Tina Marie had packed out on the blanket and he pushed his gloomy thoughts into the back of his mind while they ate. Emma was a comfortable companion for this sort of thing. He was used to women who constantly gave out the sense that they needed to be entertained. Emma wanted to talk—and actually listened to what he had to say and thought before she answered.

She was good to look at, too, from her mop of wild curls to her huge blue eyes. He liked her face, liked the way she looked as though she should have freckles scattered across her nose, liked the way her pink lips seemed to turn up at the corners. Her toes were painted pink too, a particularly happy shade of pink. The women he was used to tended to favor dark red or something more exotic and trendy, like savage blue or neon green. Pink—a color for children and stuffed animals.

That almost made him smile, so he frowned fiercely, heading the impulse off at the pass. It was little things like that that caught you up in emotional nets you didn't want to get trapped in.

They finished the food and were leaning back on the blanket, enjoying the beautiful panoramic view. He'd managed to engineer things so that his head ended up in her lap and, after a short hesitation, she began to comb her fingers through his thick hair.

Heaven, he decided, must be a lot like this.

"Tina Marie is worried about you," she said after a few minutes of silence.

"No need to be," he muttered sleepily.

"Are you angry with your brother for putting you in this position?" she asked him.

He grunted. "'Angry' doesn't do it justice. I'm damn mad at him. Here I had this lovely life laid out before me, no responsibilities to speak of, except for the duty to be happy most of the time and stay out of any major scandal. And then Julius flips out." He sighed. "I still can't believe he gave it all up…"

"For love."

"I guess that's right."

He sounded cynical and she looked down at him.

"Don't you believe in love?"

"I don't know. Do you?"

She stared at him as though no one had ever asked her that before.

"You know, I'm not really sure," she said slowly. "I'll have to get back to you on that one."

He chuckled. "Well, wherever Julius is today, I hope he's miserable," he said. "Just think of it. If it hadn't been for him, I could be in the Caribbean right now. Why couldn't I be king of a nice tropical island in the Caribbean?"

She laughed softly, enjoying the picture that concept conjured up. "Who knows? Maybe you can trade with one of the island's leaders. Put an ad in the paper."

"Right." He sighed. "It's going to be hard adjusting to living here after the lifestyle I'm used to."

She made a face. "Maybe we can bring in a beauty queen or two to keep you amused," she said, a bit of acid spicing her tone.

"Oh, you're going to start stocking them, are you? Like flour and sugar? What a good idea. I may start liking it here again after all."

She gave him a playful rub on the head and he laughed. Reaching up, he touched her cheek, then gazed at her for a moment.

"Tell me, Emma. Why don't you wear makeup?"

He thought she might take offense, but she didn't. Looking down, she answered him honestly.

"Makeup is a mask. An artifice to hide behind. I'd rather people deal with the real me." She bit her lip, wondering if he was going to buy that.

She knew her sister Rachel wouldn't. *That's a bunch of malarkey*, she would probably say. *You're just afraid to try to attract men.*

And she *was* afraid—that Rachel might have a point.

"The real you," he was repeating with a touch of mockery in his tone. He frowned, thinking about what she'd said for a moment. "I don't look at makeup that way," he said at last. "It seems to me it's a way to point out your best features. Makeup says, 'Hey, look at this. I've got eyes, and they're pretty damn good ones.'"

She laughed softly. He and Rachel would probably get along, if they ever met. "If you think it's so great, why don't *you* wear it?"

"Oh, I have."

"What?"

He laughed. "Emma, you're so easy to shock."

"I'm not." She went back to running her fingers through his hair and trying not to spend too much time staring down at the way his thick, gorgeous eyelashes shadowed his eyes. "So you think I'd look better with makeup?"

"I think you look beautiful just the way you are."

She groaned. "I wasn't fishing for compliments. 'Beautiful' is not a word that is often associated with me."

He half rose, leaning back and frowning at her. "What are you talking about?"

"Oh, please." She turned her face away.

He'd never known a woman so clueless about her looks. It made him angry to think of what someone must have said to her when she was very young to bring on such strong resistance to reality.

His gaze slid down to take in her long, shapely legs, her rounded hips and the soft, sweet swell of her breasts. His body reacted quickly and strongly and he had to change his position so she wouldn't notice.

"Emma, you bloom like a rose. Roses don't need makeup either. I only mentioned it because it interests me that you are so different from the women I'm used to."

"The women you date?"

"Yes."

"Well, I'm not a woman you date. And I never would be."

Groaning, he fell back onto the blanket. "Here we go again. The prince and the little pauper."

"The prince and the scullery maid," she corrected, glad to get off the subject of beauty. "Tell me what Tina Marie was talking about. Are you really considering not becoming king?"

"I don't know," he said lazily. "What do you think?"

She thought for a moment, then nodded. "I definitely think you should be king."

"Why?" He raised an eyebrow as though he'd got her now.

But she surprised him—she actually had a reason.

"You're a man with talent and drive. You could do big things. Cruising the Caribbean might be fun but it won't challenge you, it won't let you fulfill your potential. The country needs you, but you need the job as well."

He stared at her for so long she was afraid she'd offended him, but when he finally spoke there wasn't any evidence of it.

"What do you know about kings and what the job is like?"

"We've got our own royalty in Great Britain."

"Yes, but they're not quite as hands-on as we are here."

"Maybe you should change that."

He laughed at her. "You know what? You're beginning to sound like a woman who would love to be the power behind the throne."

"What? That's ridiculous."

"Is it?" He grinned at her. "At any rate, I think being king will work out well for me, if I do it. You know what they say—if you can fake sincerity, you've got it made in the shade."

"Well, at least you're probably cynical enough to be a monarch," she said, rolling her eyes.

"At any rate, the autopsy report should be in by

the time we get back to the castle. That will help me make up my mind. If the results are positive, I'm at least staying until I find out who killed my father."

She frowned, wondering why he was so sure his father had been assassinated. "Why would anyone have wanted to kill your father?" she asked him.

"That's always the question that lingers around royalty, isn't it? People have strange, twisted motives when they get up in the heady realms of big power. Some people go a little crazy."

Her frown deepened as she tried to think it through. "But killing him only meant Julius would be king more quickly, and it turned out he didn't want the crown."

"There you go."

"Does anyone think you did it?"

"I hardly think so. Everyone knows I'm not too enthusiastic about the royal gig."

"But if you don't do it, who else could take your place?"

"Ah. That's the rub, isn't it? It was easy enough for Julius to bug out. He knew he had me slumbering in the wings, innocent as a babe and just as clueless."

"So who comes after you?"

"Romas. A romantic lad he is, too. You might have noticed him ogling you at dinner the other night."

She scrunched her nose at him, but what he'd said had surprised her. "What about your sister?"

He shook his head. "She took herself out of the running. Maybe you haven't caught on that she's *persona non grata* around the castle. Aunt Trudy is just about the only person who even admits she exists."

To be *persona non grata* in a royal family sounded a grim fate. "What did she do?"

"You'll have to meet Agatha. I think you two will get along. Then she can tell you all about it."

It was funny, but she already liked Agatha. Just a few hours before, she'd despised her. But, as Sebastian himself had said, that was then, this was now.

"So do you suspect your cousin Romas?"

He rose to sit beside her. "Why do you ask that?"

"I don't know. Just a feeling. What does he do here, anyway?"

"That is a good question." He reached for a grape and popped it into his mouth. "Why does Romas hang around? If I do become king, I suppose I'll have to make him a minister of some sort."

"Maybe that's what he's waiting for." She frowned, considering. "Sebastian," she said, getting serious. "Is there actually going to be a coronation?"

He stared at her. "That's the first time you've called me by my name," he said softly.

"Oh, I'm sorry. I guess I should remember to use 'Your Royal Highness...'"

He took her hand in his and pressed it against his heart. "No," he said softly. "Sebastian will do."

"Okay."

Suddenly she was breathless. She'd captured his heartbeat in the palm of her hand and it sent her own heart sailing. Was he going to kiss her? She looked up into his eyes.

"Emma," he said, his voice rich and husky, "this has been an almost perfect afternoon. Only one thing could complete the perfection."

She tried to ask him what that might be but she couldn't get the words out. Her heart was thumping so hard now, she was sure he must hear it. His face lowered to hers and she closed her eyes.

His lips touched hers and she sighed, melting. She'd been kissed before. Only a few times, but there had been dates in her life. She knew about kissing. Or she'd thought she did.

But this was different from what she'd had before. This time she didn't have to wonder what to do, wonder what he wanted from her. This time, as his tongue flickered against her lips, she opened to him naturally and gasped softly as he filled her mouth with a sweet heat that traveled right down into her bloodstream and filled her body with a delicious excitement.

She could feel his interest grow. She could sense his desire stirring and knew he wanted to deepen the kiss and pull her close. But he didn't do that. He was holding back, and when he began to draw back she saw that his hands were balled into fists, as though he was forcing himself not to touch her.

She smiled at him, but deep inside she was thinking, *I could fall in love with a man like this.*

As they drove up to the back entrance to the castle Emma felt the magic of the day begin to evaporate around her.

"I'll drop you here and take the car around to the garage," he said.

She nodded. "I suppose it would be best if we weren't seen together," she said, frowning a little at the thought.

"Nonsense," he said, getting out of the car and coming around to open the door for her.

She watched him and couldn't resist a secret smile. The prince was acting the gentleman, when she was sure he was used to letting servants handle the small niceties. If he kept acting like this, she was going to have to admit how much she was starting to like him.

Rising from the seat, she thanked him, glanced at the castle doorway and said, "Nonsense or not, I'll go on in before someone sees us."

"Wait." He caught her hand and pulled her back, dropping a soft kiss on her lips. "To seal the day," he murmured, still lingering close. "Now make your run for cover."

Too late. Romas appeared, sauntering arrogantly toward them. Emma tried to pull away from Sebastian, but he was having none of it and kept her close, watching his cousin's approach with no expression on his face.

"Have a nice day?" Romas asked, looking from Sebastian to Emma and back again.

"We've had an extremely nice day," Sebastian told him. "How about you?"

Romas shrugged. "I'd say my day was more interesting than 'nice'. The final autopsy results arrived." He smiled thinly at the prince. "A clean report on all counts," he said, unable to keep a bit of triumph from his tone.

Emma could sense that Sebastian tensed, but he maintained a casual tone.

"Well, that's a relief, isn't it?" he said.

"For some of us," Romas said. "For others, I imagine it's something of a disappointment." Turning, he slipped into a small red sports car, gunned the engine and roared off toward the road.

"And good evening to you, too," Emma said tartly, watching him go. Turning to look at Sebastian, she was surprised at how brooding he looked. "Aren't you glad to find out no one was trying to poison your father?" she asked.

He glanced her way with a faint smile. "I would be glad if I was sure I believed it," he said. "I've got to get Will's thoughts on it before I can put it to rest."

"All right. I'm going in."

"All right. I'll see you later."

This time he didn't try to kiss her. There was a strange feeling in the pit of her stomach as she made her way in and then began the usual search for the right corridor. She'd had a wonderful day, but it was over. She had to be sensible about this. A relationship with Sebastian wasn't on the cards. Besides, she had a career to pursue.

That was it. She'd had her day and it was over. And that tiny crack of a heartache she could feel forming in her chest? Best to ignore it.

CHAPTER EIGHT

SEBASTIAN was waiting for Emma in the morning as she started down toward the kitchen.

"Good morning, Miss Valentine," he said, giving her a wink. "Would you please join me for a moment? I have something I need to discuss with you."

"My, how formal," she whispered as she let him escort her into a small side room and close the door.

He grinned. "I was planning to say, 'Psst, in here', but I thought better of it."

"So wise for a royal," she teased, happiness fluttering in her like a butterfly. She'd been so afraid he would act as though he didn't even know her the next time they met.

"I just wanted to let you know I'm going to be gone for a few days. Will and I are going to Zurich to talk to a specialist."

"A specialist?"

He nodded. "An authority on poisons. Will isn't satisfied with the final autopsy report and neither am I. So we're taking it to Zurich to see what an expert thinks."

"Can you just remove it like that? Will they let you?"

"Of course not." He gave her a lopsided grin. "No one wants us to take it and they are doing everything they can to stop us. But Will is busy pilfering the thing as we speak. As soon as he has it, we'll be off."

"Oh."

His eyes were sparkling and she could tell that, as seriously as he took this situation, it was also an adventure to him and he delighted in adventures. The signal from Will came in and he strode off.

She watched him go with her heart in her throat. He'd made no move to kiss her before he'd left. Not that she'd expected him to. But it did underline the fact that yesterday had been special, a day set off by itself, and not a start to anything larger.

But she'd known that. So why did she feel disappointed?

She spent the morning setting up and managing a wide inventory of all the kitchenware available, including pots and pans and small appliances. Chef Henri thought it a silly exercise, but he didn't do much beyond a sneer or two and readily let her take three of the kitchen staff to help her. Her mind kept straying every time she looked at the clock and thought, *Yesterday at this time we were running through the alleyways...* or, *This was exactly the time when Tina Marie opened her door and cried out when she saw Sebastian.*

She shook herself. She had to stop thinking like that.

"No more royalty for you!" she muttered to herself sternly as she marched off to her room for her lunch break. She was planning to delve into one of the large histories of Meridia that were sitting by her bedside.

Just before she turned the last corner, she thought she heard a child's voice, and that seemed strange. She'd noticed there didn't seem to be any children in the castle. Curious, she followed the sound around a corner and there, coming toward her on fat little unsteady bowed legs, was a toddler. He had a cute little face under a mop of red curls and it was set in determination. And not a keeper in sight.

"Hey there," she said, suddenly thinking of the nearby open stairway. She'd had enough experience with the children of friends to know a child this age needed constant supervision. "Where are you off to so quickly?"

He stopped dead, put his thumb in his mouth and stared at her, his blue eyes huge.

"Merik! Where are you? Merik!"

Sebastian's sister Agatha came barrelling into the corridor, looking anxious. "There you are," she cried, snatching the boy up into her arms. She rained kisses on his face, then beamed at Emma over his head. "Hi," she said, sticking out her hand. "I'm Agatha. And you must be Emma Valentine."

"I am."

A voice from around the corner brought an alert look into Agatha's face.

"Come on in here where we can talk without anyone seeing him," she said quickly, pushing open a door into a bedroom whose floor was covered with children's toys.

Emma followed her into the room, but she asked, "Why shouldn't anyone see him?"

Agatha set her child down and pushed back her thick hair. "He's not supposed to exist. We've been officially un-officiated, as it were. As far as this castle goes, we are non-persons, he and I."

"But...you're in the royal family."

"Come sit down," Agatha said, sitting beside her on an overstuffed couch. "And I'll try to explain." She settled back. "It's a funny thing, growing up royal. Julius was the good son and now look at him. Sebastian was the rebel, and now he's going to be king. And I…" She sighed. "I ran off to see the world and played that famous game of Stupid Princess and came back with a baby and no husband."

"Oh, I'm sorry. And the father of the baby didn't want to get married?"

"Oh, sure." Agatha laughed. "He'd have loved to marry me. How could he turn down all this?" She swept the length of the room with her hand. "But he was no prize and I was a ridiculous little idiot. My father disowned me, the country despises me and the current protectorate warned me not to darken the castle door again."

"But you're here."

"Yes." Her smile made her look positively angelic. "All because of Sebastian. He made them let me come back. And if he becomes king, I'll be back for good."

Emma smiled at her in sympathy. The father of her child was probably the man who had tried to kidnap her and been stopped by Sebastian. The pieces were all falling into place.

"Agatha, I'm so sorry you had to go through that. I know what it's like to have a father disapprove."

"You can say that, and in theory you're right. But whenever I look at that darling child, I'm sorry for all the agony I've put everyone through, but, as for me, I just can't regret a thing."

Emma watched as the princess looked lovingly at her son and she felt a pang. She'd never thought about having children herself. Her whole life had been organized around her career. Children hadn't seemed relevant. So what explained this sudden little sense of emotion she was feeling? Did falling for a man mean you suddenly wanted children, too? Was it that firmly implanted in her genetic makeup?

Not that she'd actually fallen for a man, she assured herself quickly.

"I can see that you're a wonderful mother," she told Agatha.

"I try to be. My party days are definitely over, with no regrets."

"Now you just have to find a daddy for your baby. Or is that out of the question?"

To Emma's surprise, Agatha hesitated and flushed a bit.

"Actually, I have someone in mind for that," she

said with the ghost of a smile. "Now it's just a matter of convincing him that it can work."

"Ah. Good luck."

Agatha looked at her questioningly. "So what do you think?" she asked her, leaning forward. "Is Sebastian going to do it?"

"Take the crown?" Emma was getting used to the question now. It no longer surprised her. "I think he should. What do you think?"

Agatha hesitated. "Well, he wasn't born to be king, you know. He was born and bred to be the happy-go-lucky second son—playing the horses and laying the wives. Oh, I don't mean it literally," she added quickly when she saw Emma's face. She put a comforting hand on her arm. "But that's the image the people have of him. That's the role he's been trained for."

Emma was conflicted but she felt she had to speak her piece. "I know I'm so new to this, I don't really have a right to an opinion, but I have one anyway. I think you're selling your brother short. I think he has not only the talent to be a good king, but the responsibility to do it."

A smile broke on Agatha's face and she threw her arms around Emma. "Oh, I knew I was going to like you," she cried. "That's exactly how I feel. This country is just dozing, waiting for the right leadership to bring it to life. Welcome to the conspiracy to convince him to do it."

The two of them spent another half-hour getting to know each other and making plans to talk to Sebastian. Emma was feeling very empowered by this new friendship. She knew she would never have a romantic relationship with Sebastian, but she could help him do the right thing.

"Oh, there's something I have to warn you about," Agatha said as Emma was getting up to leave. "I may not be a welcome face around here, but I still do have my sources. And the buzz is, there are a couple of people in prominent positions who are lobbying to get rid of you."

A shiver went through Emma's heart. "Why?"

"That's a good question. I'm not sure if it's because they've seen you and Sebastian together and can tell there's some sort of chemistry there—"

"That's crazy!"

"Or if his little lecture about you knowing about poisons scared someone."

"Oh, Agatha…"

"Don't let it upset you. This sort of thing is always going on around here. I just wanted to warn you to watch your step."

"I will."

And the day had been going so well up to that point. Agatha's warning put a chill on it.

The next day started well enough, and then in the afternoon the housekeeper pulled her aside, acting conspiratorial.

"I have to ask a favor of you," she said. "We have a very important dinner tomorrow night. Chef Henri, unfortunately, has been called away. His mother is ill. Could you possibly take over and handle it?"

Her spirits leaped. "Of course. I'd be happy to."

"You'll have to do everything, I'm afraid, from menu planning and ordering the supplies on down. Nothing has been done. Please understand how important this dinner is going to be. It needs to be special. Certain members of very old-fashioned, traditional factions will be in attendance. They've been very obstructionist and the prime minister is hoping they can be cajoled. As things stand right now, they are vehemently against the prince's coronation."

"Because of his playboy reputation?" Emma asked, curious.

The housekeeper hesitated, then ignored the question and went on.

"Delicate negotiations are going on right now. If anything were to go wrong with the dinner…"

"Don't worry." Emma was excited about the opportunity. "Everything will go like clockwork. I guarantee it."

"All right. Now remember, they are traditional. Nothing too trendy on the menu, please."

Nothing too trendy. Okay. How about roast beef? And for the fish course…a bright idea suddenly occurred to her. Why not the unicomus, the fish she'd seen in the market the day before? Oh, my. She smiled just thinking of it. She'd won a prize at a competition in Belgium with her version of Monkfish Tournedos on a bed of Caramelized Langoustines. The unicomus would be perfect for something similar. She knew just how she would handle the presentation. And with those wonderful faces, a large, grilled unicomus spread out on a platter would make a spectacular centerpiece for that course—and be symbolic for the hope of Meridia being united behind Sebastian.

Wow. It was exciting to think that her cuisine could be a part of Meridian diplomacy.

She went to work on it right away. When she gave the supply list to the kitchen boy who was being sent into town to do the shopping, he looked it over and then gave her a puzzled look.

"Is there something you don't understand?" she asked him.

He hesitated, then shook his head, but he stopped to show the list to Angela, the prep cook who had been particularly antagonistic to Emma. That made her curious and she was about to ask them what the problem was when she noticed Agatha sneaking into the pantry to look for snacks for her baby, and she forgot all about it as she made a show of casually going into the pantry herself, in order to help her.

It was nice to have a friend at the castle. But she didn't have much of a chance to spend time with her. She was so busy preparing for the big dinner, she didn't even have time to miss Sebastian, though she did pause now and then to wonder how his meeting with the specialist had gone.

The next day she was totally immersed in preparations, from food to the table setting, and she was surprised when someone mentioned that Sebastian had returned the night before. That made her wonder why he hadn't said hello. But she assumed he was as wrapped up in his project as she was in hers.

She saw him early in the afternoon, looking things over and ordering the wine to be brought from the wine cellar, but he was in a different room talking with the sommelier and didn't look up when she passed.

That disturbed her a little, but she didn't have time to think about it. She was intent on doing such a good job that he would be proud to have her as his coronation chef. And if her meal could help him with his diplomacy, so much the better. The kitchen was a madhouse, but she was keeping a cool head and things seemed to be falling into place.

She took a short break late in the afternoon. She'd promised Agatha that she would come up and visit for a while, but she really didn't have time for that. Still, she thought she would stop by for a minute or two.

But when she knocked, it was a male voice that called out, "Help!"

Startled, she opened the door and stepped in, only to find Sebastian on his back on the floor, with Merik happily using his chest as a trampoline.

"Thank God," he said when he saw her.

"What are you doing?"

He frowned. "Babysitting is harder to get right than you'd think," he said sheepishly. "This kid's got me pinned to the floor. Can you get him? I don't want to knock him down and hurt him."

"Sure." She took the gurgling boy up into her arms. His fat little limbs went wild and she could hardly hold him. "I see what you mean," she said, laughing as Sebastian rose to a sitting position, then stood. "Here, have him back."

The prince took the child, hugged him to his chest and murmured sweet nothings for a moment, kissed the top of his downy head, then set him into his playpen. Merik promptly settled back against a pillow, closed his eyes and went to sleep.

"Wow," Emma said, watching in awe. "You're going to make a great dad."

Sebastian was staring at the child, too. "Is this for real?" he said suspiciously. "Are you sure he isn't trying to trick me?"

She laughed, turning toward him and he caught hold of her.

"Hey, I missed you," he said, and the next thing she knew he was kissing her.

His body was hard and wonderful against her breasts and her hips and his mouth was so hot, she was breathless. But she couldn't let this happen.

"No," she said, leaning away. "No, Sebastian, not in front of the child."

He pulled her back and buried his face in her thick, curly hair, laughing softly. "What's the matter? You think the kid's going to squeal?" he asked.

She shook her head and pried his arms from around her. "I've got to go back. I only stopped in to see Agatha for a minute because I'd promised I would."

Reluctantly, he let her go. "So you're in charge of dinner tonight?"

She nodded.

"Is it going to be great?"

She nodded again.

He grinned. "Good. I'm holding you to that."

She started toward the door, then looked back. "And your trip to Zurich?" she asked.

He waved her on. "I'll tell you about it later," he said. "Go be a genius of a chef."

"Okay."

His eyes were deep with a warmth that thrilled her and her heart sang as she left him. She wouldn't let herself think about the long term. No point to it. The short term would do—for now.

The company assembled on the terrace and an hour later they were summoned into the dining hall. Emma made a last-minute survey of the table and then stood back and watched for a moment as the diners arrived. She thought she could tell those who belonged to the traditional bunch who didn't like Sebastian. Most were elegantly attired, the men in tuxedos, the women in long gowns, but three men and two women were dressed in traditional Meridian costume. They had to be the ones everyone was especially anxious to impress and satisfy.

Once again Sebastian failed to look her way, but she refused to let herself dwell on it. She had things to do.

The soup went out and the empty bowls came back with compliments to the chef that made her glow. And now the fish course was served, with two footmen carrying out the huge grilled unicomus on the platter for the centerpiece. Emma got busy on the main course, a beautiful roast beef with truffles and kohlrabi, cooked to perfection. She was carefully arranging slices on a plate when she first began to realize something was wrong.

A shout from the dining hall was her first clue, then a clash of voices getting louder and louder. Frowning, she put down her knife and wiped her hands on her apron, starting toward the door.

She hadn't taken two steps when the door burst open from the other side and the short, stout prime minister came roaring in.

"What in God's name do you think you're doing?" he shouted at her, waving his arms. "Are you mocking us and our traditions?"

"What?" Stunned, she was at a loss.

"It's an outrage, a sacrilege!"

Another man who was a stranger to her came striding in behind him. "You'll pay for this, young lady," he said, shaking his finger at her. "I swear, you'll pay."

She shook her head, her hand to her throat. "I…I'm sorry, I have no idea what you're talking about. What have I done?"

"The unicomus. How could you?"

"The fish? But—"

"The unicomus is our national fish. It is sacred to us. We never, never eat it."

"What?" Horror shot through her like an electric shock. Such a thing had never occurred to her. "But…but why didn't anyone…?"

Her voice trailed off as she looked about the kitchen. It was strangely empty. Everyone had fled and left her alone to face this. They'd known it was coming. That was why no one had told her. Because they hadn't wanted her to know until it was too late.

She turned back, her heart leaden. "Oh, dear. I'm so sorry. I didn't know."

"Didn't know? Didn't know? That's a lame excuse."

"But no one…"

She stopped herself. No, she wasn't going to blame this on anyone else. She should have researched it more fully. She knew most of the kitchen staff was out to get her. She should have checked.

"I'm just so sorry," she said quickly. "This is completely my responsibility. Please. Let me go out and apologize to everyone."

She made her way out to the head of the table, her heart beating like thunder in her chest. Public speaking was not her forte, but this had to be done.

Sebastian rose as she approached the table. That pulse at his temple was throbbing hard. Her gaze met his and she didn't see anything friendly there. Did he think she'd done this on purpose?

Well, she had. She'd wanted to surprise him— never a good idea. There was a horrible, hollow feeling where her pride and happiness were supposed to be. She stopped beside him and turned to face the diners.

"Please, may I have your attention? I'm Emma Valentine. I was the head chef for your meal tonight."

"You should be ashamed," a thin, silver-haired woman in traditional costume cried.

"Take your haute-cuisine style back to wherever you came from," a dark man chimed in. "We don't need your kind here in Meridia."

She swallowed hard and squared her shoulders as she looked out at the angry faces.

"Please listen to me. I knew that the unicomus is your national fish. I knew of the great affection all people of Meridia hold for this animal. What I didn't know was..." She gestured toward the table. "I didn't realize it was held in such high esteem that it was never eaten. That I didn't know."

There was a murmur of disbelief.

"But you see, my dear," Aunt Trudy chided gently, "here in Meridia, we are all raised with so many stories about the unicomus. He is our folklore, he is our ancestor, he is our hero. It is the unicomus who saves children from drowning, who saves kittens from being eaten by nastier fish, who warns the sailor of coming storms. He is our dearest pet and he embodies the national spirit. To eat him would be...a form of cannibalism."

More mutterings of agreement came from the diners.

"Your Highness, I truly didn't understand that. I am so, so sorry." She looked back at the others. "If you can't forgive me, at least please understand, I didn't know."

"Well, it was beautifully prepared, my dear," said Aunt Trudy diplomatically. "Perhaps another time with a different fish."

She tried to smile. "I'll have something else brought out to you right away, if you can just indulge me for ten minutes."

She glanced at Sebastian for the first time since she'd started speaking. His face was impassive. She had no idea what he was thinking.

"And once again, ladies and gentlemen," she said as she turned to go, "my abject apologies."

She strode quickly back toward the kitchen. Tears threatened, but only for a few seconds. She let her anger back in to keep them at bay. She would certainly like to wring some necks. No wonder the staff had headed for the tall grass.

Sebastian came in right behind her, grabbing her arm to pull her around to face him.

"What were you thinking?" he demanded.

She looked up at him and wanted more than anything to be in his arms. But he wasn't in that sort of mood. Here she'd worked so hard to impress him and make him proud, and instead she'd ruined everything. But that didn't mean she was going to crumble.

"You tell me this," she said right back. "Why were those unicornus fish being sold in the market if nobody eats them? What is that all about?"

He blinked. "We don't eat them. Italians do. It's a delicacy. They come up on purpose to buy them."

She shook her head in disbelief. "Let me get this straight. They are too sacred to eat, but not too sacred to sell to Italians to eat. Is that it?"

"Don't ask for logic, Emma," he said. "It's always been done that way. What can I tell you?"

Closing her eyes, she shook her head. "What you could have told me is, 'Don't ever cook that fish'."

He frowned. "Wait a minute, Emma. Are you telling me that no one in the kitchen warned you? No one said a word?"

She hesitated. She was afraid she knew where this was going and that was only going to make things worse. Much as she would like to punish a few of the kitchen staff herself, she didn't want the prince to get involved.

"No one said anything," she admitted. "But it's my own fault for not—"

He swore angrily, his face dark. "I'll fire every one of them."

"No!"

"Of course I will. They must have done this deliberately."

"I'm sure they did. But you can't fire them. I'm going to need every one of them for the coronation dinner." She looked up into his eyes, wishing he would take down the ice-cold barrier that kept her from seeing what he was thinking. "Besides, they deserve a little leeway on this. It's been coming for a long time. They finally got back at me."

His brows drew together. "What are you talking about?"

She shook her head. "They've all resented me from the moment I arrived. You can hardly blame them. They were, in effect, being told they weren't good enough to pull off the coronation dinner. That they needed me to come in and tell them what to do in their own kitchen. Naturally, they wanted to see me stumble."

He stared down at her for a long moment. For just a second or two she thought his stone-cold eyes were softening. But it didn't last. Shaking his head, he swore again and turned on his heel, heading back out to the dining hall.

Meanwhile, Emma began to scramble to put together something to take the place of the fish course. One by one, the kitchen staff straggled back in, looking shamefaced and getting right to work without a word. She acted as though nothing had happened as well, and the rest of the evening went beautifully.

But always in the back of her mind was a new ugly fear. After what Agatha had told her about people wanting her gone, this episode should have put the icing on the cake. If anyone was going to be fired, it was probably her.

And she had a hard time looking that possibility straight in the eye. There would be the disappointment, of course. The blow to her career. The humiliation as the look on her father's face said, "I told you so."

But the worst result would be something completely new. If she were fired, she knew without a doubt she would never see Sebastian again.

CHAPTER NINE

EMMA opened her eyes in the morning and wished hard that everything that had happened the day before had been a dream, something she could laugh off. But the hollow ache in the pit of her stomach told her otherwise. She could only hope that this day would be better.

Unfortunately, pieces of bad news seemed to be lining up to take turns tormenting her. After dressing, she went down to the kitchen and the first thing she saw was the local newspaper spread out on the kitchen table. There was a large, fuzzy picture of a couple in the midst of a gentle kiss on the cover, and the headline read, MONTY KISSES TRAITOR CHEF.

She gasped and her stomach did a somersault. Shaking, she pushed the paper away and turned, getting to work. It was all she could think to do.

The kitchen staff were on their best behavior today. The night before, after all the guests had gone, Sebastian had come in, gathered them together, and let them have it.

"That was a nasty trick you played tonight," he told them angrily. "By rights I should sack you all. I fully intended to do so. But now I've been told that would be a mistake. In other words, you are all very good at what you do and we need you. At least for the short term. So you have a reprieve. No one is to be sacked until after the coronation."

Gasps were heard all around.

"And maybe not even then. But that will depend on your behavior. You'll be watched. And just to make it easier, you'll each take turns doing the watching and I want a report on how things went every evening."

That was such a smart thing he'd done—getting them to report on each other rather than giving her the duty. That way, they couldn't see her as the bad guy. Sebastian was impressing her with his management skills.

But she hadn't impressed much of anyone herself. And now she would have to make up for it.

It was an hour or so later that she began to hear the shouting from the breakfast room and she knew it had to be over the news story. Heart racing, she tried to come up with a plan. This was such a nightmare. She hated to think her mistake was causing Sebastian so much trouble. What could she do?

She knew what she could do. She could leave. Pain stabbed her soul at the thought. But that way she could quit being a problem for Sebastian.

She closed her eyes and gathered all the courage she had left. Then she headed for the breakfast room.

Morning light streamed in from the high windows set all around. A sideboard groaned under the weight of bacon, sausages, scrambled eggs, pancakes, and every other breakfast food imaginable. But no one was eating.

The eight men and two women scattered around the circular table fell silent, watching her. The animosity was so thick in the air, it could have been a fog. Taking a deep breath, she faced them all.

"I'm here to tender my resignation," she said, amazed that her voice sounded so calm.

"What a relief," said the finance minister, throwing up his hands.

"Wonderful," said one of the women.

"That will surely help a lot," said one of the men.

It looked as though they were in complete

agreement and the angry faces were beginning to
soften a bit. The only one who hadn't reacted was
Sebastian. He was half leaning, half sitting on a
counter along the back of the room, his arms
folded across his chest.

"I'm sure Chef Henri can handle the coronation
dinners," she said, fighting back the stinging in
her eyes. "You have a good staff. You'll be okay."
She didn't dare meet Sebastian's gaze. If she did,
she knew the tears would start to flow and she
would die first.

"I'll pack my things and be out before lunch,"
she said, working hard to keep her voice from
shaking. She'd just begun to turn back toward the
door when Sebastian finally spoke.

"No," he said simply. "You're not going anywhere."

She risked a quick look his way. His face was
still set in stone.

"Your Royal Highness, I think you have
enough problems without me cluttering things
up. What I did last night was unforgivable. It's
only right that I—"

"What you did last night you were tricked into
doing by a vindictive staff," he said firmly. "I
won't have you punished for what others caused."

"But what about the newspapers?" a cabinet

minister insisted, pointing to the local rag someone had spread out in the middle of the table. "What about this picture?"

"There's been too much scandal as it is," another chimed in. "You know, we were afraid of this when we found out you were going to take the crown. We can't have things like this happening all the time. We're the laughingstock of Europe."

"Oh, why did Julius have to leave us?" a plaintive voice said softly.

Emma licked her dry lips. "Your Highness, if you please. I really think it would be better if I left. You have a country to run. It's so important that you think of your country first."

Sebastian heard her words but he gave no indication of his reaction. Slowly, he looked around the table, examining each person, one by one. These were all high-ranking, celebrated men and women who planned to spend most of their time eating his food, vying for his favor. When he became king, these people would be his constant companions. They weren't friends he would have chosen for himself. There weren't many he trusted. Just looking at them made him want to throw it all in and run for the hills—or rather the warm waters of the Caribbean.

He thought of the old days when his father had

presided over this same bunch, before he'd fallen ill and begun to slowly wither away. Did one of these people have a hand in hurrying his father's demise? He wished he knew the truth.

Finally, he looked at Emma. She wasn't royal. She wasn't from one of the finer families in Meridia. She wasn't even one of the brainless beauties he was used to having around. But one thing he was sure of: she was honest as the day was long. Looking around the table, he realized that she was probably the only person present he could really trust.

And they wanted him to throw her away? Not a chance.

"I'd like you all to leave now," he said evenly. "Except you, Emma. I want to talk to you."

Romas rose, looking insolent. "Do you really think that's a good idea?" he asked, giving Emma a sideways glance that was an airborne insult.

Sebastian sighed. He was going to have to give Romas his comeuppance at some point. Better sooner than later, he supposed, but he wasn't quite ready to do it yet.

"I think it's the best idea I've had in days," he said. "Get out, Romas."

As the room emptied he turned to Emma, but he purposely kept distance between them.

"Come sit down," he said, dropping into a chair at the table himself.

She sat down across from him, watching him intently, her eyes huge. Obviously, she didn't know what to expect. Something told him she often expected the worst. He pushed that thought away because it made him want to pull her into his arms.

"You're going to stay," he told her firmly. "You signed a contract and I'm not letting you out of it."

She drew in a sharp breath. "I meant what I said," she told him. "You have to concentrate on preparing to be king. You don't need your life cluttered up with problems. I'm just so sorry—"

"Will you cut that out? You've said your piece. I know how you feel about that. What I want to know is…all things being equal, do you want to stay?"

Conflicting emotions flickered across her face, but in the end she nodded.

"Good. You're my anchor right now, Emma. That may sound strange to you, but the thing is you're one of the few people I think I can rely on. And that makes you very valuable to me."

"Oh. Well. I…I'm glad." She looked a bit puzzled, but willing.

"But at the same time…" He grimaced and looked away. "I had a long talk with Will on our trip to Zurich. He made me face some home truths."

"Like what?"

He looked back at her, studying her adorable face and those inviting lips. "I had a wonderful time with you the other day. It was one of the best days of my life. I just want you to know that be-cause…we can't do it again."

She nodded, trying so hard to keep her dignity, her distance, while at the same time her big blue eyes were filling with tragedy. "I understand. And I agree."

"In a way, this is a sort of goodbye. We'll still be seeing each other all the time. But we won't…" He grimaced again, unable to think of words to describe what he meant.

But she knew.

He shifted his position and took a deep breath. His gaze fell on the newspaper in the center of the table and he reached for it.

"Can you believe this awful picture? Someone caught us on a telephoto lens. Didn't I warn you about the media?"

He saw the pain in her face. She felt betrayed and violated by knowing someone had been taking pictures of their wonderful day. He knew how she felt. He felt the same way. And he was used to it.

"And they already knew about the fish disaster. But to call me a traitor!"

"You'll get called worse."

She looked wounded, then shook it away.

"What happened in Zurich?" she asked, as though she really needed to change the subject quickly.

"We took the report and a few samples to the specialist. He's looking them over and running a few tests himself. It will take a little time before he can give us an answer. But from what we told him and what he saw, he has doubts, just like Will did."

She shook her head. "I don't know whether to hope for bad news or good," she said.

He smiled at her. "It is a bit of a muddle, isn't it?"

His smile faded as he took in her earnest goodness. He couldn't help himself. He had to reach out to her. He put his hand out, stretching his arm across the table, and after a slight hesitation she met it with her own. Their fingers laced together and their gazes held for a long, long moment.

And he thought again, was the effort, and all he had to give up, worth the prize?

The next few days went by quickly, although there was a hint of melancholy to everything Emma did. Just as the prince had said, they saw each other often, but almost every time they met or passed one another in the hallway they avoided eye contact. The few times that their gazes did meet, something secret seemed to pass between them. Emma wasn't sure just what it was, but it made her pulse go wild every time.

In the meantime, she and Agatha were becoming good friends. She usually stopped by to see Agatha and play with Merik at least once a day. And twice she'd seen Will Harris leaving Agatha's room. An idea was beginning to dawn on her. Could Dr Will be the man Agatha had in mind as Merik's father?

Oh, she hoped so! That would be perfect.

"Perfect? Are you kidding?" Agatha protested when she tentatively brought it up. "Of course Will is the man. I've been in love with him since I was about fifteen. He's always been a good friend of Sebastian's. But his father was a landscaper in charge of the castle gardens and he thinks that means we can't be together. I say, 'rubbish!' to that."

Emma laughed. "I can imagine you do."

"He's got his pride, you know. And plans to emigrate to South America." Agatha rolled her eyes. "No, that is not on the cards. I want him right here, married to me."

"How are you planning to make that happen?"

"I don't know. Once we convince Sebastian to take the crown, we can get started on convincing Will that I'm a woman, not a princess."

If it hadn't been for Agatha, she would have felt very isolated, because she was having trouble getting in touch with anyone back in London. Her cousin Louise in particular was strangely unavailable. Emma hadn't been able to contact her for days.

And when they finally did connect, she found out what the problem was.

"Oh, Emma, I've been dying to talk to you," Louise said when she finally responded to one of Emma's calls.

"Then why don't you ever answer your phone?" Emma asked, sensibly.

"I couldn't. I've been too upset, too confused to talk to anyone. Something's happened."

Emma immediately went on alert. "What?"

"Don't worry, nobody died or anything like that. Well, my father did have a slight heart attack. My father—hah!"

"Uncle John had a heart attack? Oh, Louise, I'm so sorry. How is he?"

"I don't know. Oh, he's okay, but I'm not speaking to either of my parents at the moment."

"Louise, will you explain what's going on?" As an only child, Louise was the most beloved, cosseted—one might even say, spoiled—person Emma knew. For her to be angry with her parents was unheard of.

"I'll tell you what's going on. My parents have lied to me for years. Did you know I was adopted? I keep wondering if everyone knew but me. Did you know?"

Emma was at a loss. "What do you mean, you're adopted? How can that be?"

"How indeed."

"Are you sure?"

"Oh, yes. It all came out when a couple of my father's illegitimate children showed up on the doorstep. Twins, Daniel and Dominic. Mother's having DNA tests run, but it's hardly necessary. They are the spitting image. Which made me wonder why I'd never noticed that I'm not. So now, I'm the odd man out."

Emma could hear the pain in her voice, despite her attempts to treat the situation facetiously.

"Louise, you know that your parents adore you."

"They did. As long as I was in the dark about things. Now that I know everything, there's this horrible wall between us." Louise's voice broke and she paused for a moment to regain her composure. "I...I feel like I've lost everything."

"Oh, Louise, surely not. I know your parents love you. And if they adopted you, they've proved it. They chose you—"

"Oh, sure. Nice try, Emma. I'm not buying it. I've applied at an agency to find my real birth mother. Hopefully, she's not a liar, too."

"Louise!"

"And now my parents are as angry at me as I am at them. They don't even want to speak to me. They think I'm betraying them by trying to find my birth mother." Her voice broke again. "Oh, Emma, it's all such a mess."

"Do you need me to come there? You know, I wouldn't be able to stay long, but I could catch a flight out and—"

"No. No. But you're a sweetheart to offer. There's no point coming here, because I'm leaving. I've got to get out of here."

"Well, why don't you come here, then?" Emma said, suddenly excited by the idea. "I'm sure I can arrange a room for you."

"You know what? I just might do that. Have

you got any spare princes hanging around? I could use a fling with royalty to cheer me up."

Emma coughed. "Sorry. The one we've got is busy."

"Still doing his Hamlet act, huh?"

Emma had hinted that Sebastian was not sold on taking over as king and Louise had been taken by the idea of someone who didn't grab power when he had the chance.

"Oh, well. I'm having my own crisis so I guess I won't try to horn in on his. I'll let you know when I can arrange to come. And, Emma—thank you just for being there. I was in real need of a friendly voice."

"Any time. You know that."

She hung up with a sigh. It was instructive to be reminded that others had problems, too, sometimes a lot worse than yours.

The parties meant to introduce Sebastian to eligible young ladies had begun. The first was a dinner for a dozen beauties, the second an evening of music and poetry reading with another twenty.

"The point of that," Duchess Trudy had told Emma with a sparkle in her eye, "is to see who falls asleep from boredom. We do want a queen who can hold her own with the cultured crowd."

"What makes you think the prince will last the evening?" Emma said with a grin.

Trudy waved a hand dismissively. "Doesn't matter. Men get dispensation from such things. But we must have some standards for our queen. She can't be just anyone, you know."

Oh, yes, she knew that only too well.

The next affair was a culmination of the search, scheduled two nights on. A ball was planned, with a dinner before the dancing and a midnight dessert buffet table. She threw herself into the task just as she threw herself into everything these days. But she couldn't help but think she was probably making something delicious for the woman Sebastian would marry. That was a depressing thought.

The day was hot and muggy. Meridia was undergoing the last heat wave of the summer and it was pretty miserable, especially working in the kitchen. She was blocking out the pastry squares for the desserts when she looked up to see Sebastian passing through. No one else was nearby and he paused as he came next to her.

"Meet me in the first-floor library in ten minutes," he whispered.

He left before she could say a word. Her mouth went dry and she tried to keep her hands from trembling as she finished her work, washed her hands, and started for the library.

Stepping out into the main corridor, she saw Romas and the prime minister coming her way. Romas' head rose as he noticed her and she had a sense that he would try to waylay her when they passed one another. That was certainly something she wanted to avoid. Ducking into a storage closet, she held her breath until they'd passed. Thankfully, Romas didn't come looking for her. She counted to twenty-five, then carefully opened the door and peeked out. The corridor was empty.

The library, once she'd reached it, seemed dark and empty as well. She closed the door and looked around, and suddenly Sebastian appeared from behind another door.

"Oh," she said, slightly startled. "Hello."

"Hello." He smiled at her. "Do you know how cute you look in that crazy white cooking outfit?"

"Sebastian!" she admonished, coloring and pleased as Punch. She'd never realized before how wonderful it was to have someone happy to see you.

"I'm sorry. I just couldn't resist." He sobered and gestured for her to sit down on a nearby chair. He dropped down onto the arm of the leather couch.

"Okay, I asked you to meet with me because I thought you might want to know how things are going on the poison front."

"Of course. Did you get answers from the specialist in Zurich?"

"Of a sort. He agrees that there seems to be some cause for suspicion. Certain elements of my father's condition correlate with the effects of a slow poisoning."

"Oh, Sebastian!"

"The problem is pinning down what agent might have been used. It's difficult to test for something if you don't know what you're testing for."

"I see."

"So we're not much closer to a solution, but we're more sure than ever that something was being done to him."

She nodded, knowing that it was a result he'd expected, yet dreaded at the same time. "What's your next move?"

"I wish I knew. Will is looking into a few possibilities. We'll see if he can dig anything up. In the meantime…" He shrugged.

"It's less than a week until the coronation," she said. That meant only a little over a week until her job here was over. Her mind shied away from that.

"Yes," he said.

She searched his eyes but there were no answers there. So she asked him directly. "Are you prepared to go through with it?"

He sighed. "That's still the dilemma I wrestle with." He paused, then went on.

"You do understand what's involved, don't you? On the day of the coronation, for me, all normal life will cease for ever. Every single move I make, every word I speak, will be pinned to the wall and examined, criticized and scorned, printed and reprinted and reanalyzed in case another reason for despising me can be found. I'm not used to that. I don't really want to get used to it. And that's only one of the things I would hate about this job."

He moved restlessly. "You realize, as a young man, I got out of here as soon as I could and I haven't regretted that for a moment."

"But, Sebastian..." She leaned forward earnestly. "Yes, it will make drastic changes in your lifestyle. But that only underlines the fact that this is a very important job. You can't trivialize it."

She wished she could think of better words to help persuade him.

"The future of this country, whether it will grow and flourish, and the welfare of a couple of million people—is on your shoulders. Whatever you do, you can't let them down."

He stared at her, looking bemused. "Why do you care?"

She sat back again and looked away. "I don't know. I just think you…well, you have such an opportunity here. You shouldn't waste it."

He smiled at her. "You may be right," he said, but he didn't sound convinced.

She looked down at her hands in order to stay away from his gaze. Those golden eyes had rocked her world from the first, and they hadn't lost their power with familiarity.

"I'd better get back," she said, rising from the chair.

"Yes," he said, rising as well.

She hesitated. She hated to leave. They had so few moments together. And there was something she wanted to know.

"Well, have you chosen a potential queen as yet?" she asked brightly, not sure she was allowed to broach this subject, but doing it anyway.

When he didn't answer right away, she looked up into his eyes to see why. His smile had faded and his eyes darkened.

"What do you think?" he asked her softly.

Suddenly she noticed that his knuckles were

white where he held the back of the chair and she had the fantastic thought that maybe he was having a hard time keeping himself from coming to take her in his arms. Her heart leaped, even though she knew that was too outlandish to be true. Still, she turned quickly.

"I'd better get back," she said again.

"Yes," he agreed. "You'd better go."

At the doorway she turned and looked back at him. Was it just her imagination, or were his eyes haunted? Turning away, she left quickly. She didn't want him to see the tears trembling in her own eyes.

CHAPTER TEN

EMMA was having trouble sleeping again. She'd almost forgotten how impossible sleep had been when she'd first arrived. That problem had vanished once Dr Will had taken her in hand. But now it was back.

And tonight was the worst. The heat was suffocating. Not even the tiniest breeze moved her white window curtains. After two hours of tossing and turning, she gave up.

"I thought these old castles with their high ceilings were built to be cool in the summer and snug in the winter," she muttered resentfully. "Can we join the modern age now? Where's the air-conditioning!"

Slipping into shorts and a light jersey top, she grabbed her robe and opened her door as quietly as she could, making her way out into the hall. She knew where she wanted to go: the only cool place she'd found in the building—the swimming pool.

She'd pretty much learned to find her way around the castle by now, and she headed straight for the pool. The door clanked a bit, making her shudder, but the cavernous area was dark and empty, just as she'd hoped it would be. No one was here. She could lie down on one of the benches and maybe, just maybe, she would sleep.

She sat at the side of the pool for a while first, dangling her feet in the cool water and trying to remember everything that had happened that first day when she'd known Sebastian as Monty and he'd stayed with her for so long. Memories were fuzzy. She'd spent a lot of that time only half awake. But the things she did remember made her smile.

She dampened down her shorts and top and went looking for a bench suitable for sleeping on. She found one tucked away in a corner, protected by an overhang. She was just settling down, using a pair of handy water wings for a pillow, when the door clanged open again. She froze. Someone was coming in. She held her breath.

A male form was walking toward the edge of the pool. He dove in without hesitation, but she could see it was Sebastian. He began to do laps, swimming back and forth, back and forth. She watched for a few minutes, impressed with him as she always was. He swam beautifully, his stroke elegant and graceful, but with explosive power—just like his beautiful, powerful body.

She bit her lip, wondering what to do. She had three choices. She could lie down and sleep in this hidden place and he would probably never know she was there. Or she could slink out quietly and he would probably never know she'd been there. Or she could be honest and straightforward and go down on the pool deck and let him know she was here. What to do? What to do?

But she was already doing it—no choice involved. Gathering her robe and her water wings, she made her way down to the side of the pool and spread out, lying down and listening to the rhythmic sound of his swimming. In mere moments, she was sound asleep.

"Oh, my God, not again."

She opened her eyes to find him standing over her, dripping water and gazing in astonishment.

"I swear I didn't even touch a water-polo ball," he said.

She smiled and moved lazily. "And this time I was here first," she noted. "*You're* the one who came to join *me*."

He had only a trace of a smile. "What are you doing here?" he asked.

"Looking for a cool place to sleep. This castle is like an oven. I recommend that the first thing you do after you put that crown on your head is to call up some workers and put air-conditioning in this place."

He chuckled, then dropped down beside her on the deck, sitting cross-legged. "Seems like old times," he said. "Haven't we met this way before?"

"I seem to remember something like this. Long ago and far away."

Reaching out, he took her hand in his and began to play with her fingers. She watched, loving the way his cool hand felt against her warm skin.

"How did you get to be such a good swimmer?" she asked lazily.

"There was a time when I was young that I used swimming to calm down. I felt like everything and everyone was against me and I would take out my frustrations in the water, hour after hour. Along the way, I got good at it."

She frowned, looking at his handsome face. People so blessed with beauty and wealth and position were supposed to be happy ever after. "Why were you so frustrated?"

He thought for a moment, looking at her.

"Julius was so good at everything," he told her at last. "And everyone praised him all the time. I was the awkward one, the chunky one, the kid who didn't quite fit in."

She looked at him in disbelief. "You?"

His grin was lopsided. "Yes, Emma. I wasn't always the magnificent specimen you see before you now." He said it in a mocking, self-effacing way, but that didn't really work when you looked as good as he did.

"Hard to believe," she murmured.

If he really wanted to see someone who felt unloved and unappreciated, he should time-travel back to her childhood. But she frowned, chastising herself for thinking that. After all, everyone's private hell was his own and couldn't be compared to anyone else's. To him, what he'd endured must have felt just as unbearable as her unhappiness had felt to her.

Without thinking, she reached out and stopped a large drop of water that was running down the tan skin of his thigh, catching it on her finger. She knew right away that she shouldn't have done it, but, for some reason, she didn't care.

"Your skin feels so cool," she said softly, reaching for another drop that was slowly making its way down his chest.

She saw his stomach muscles contract and she looked up into his eyes. She wanted...something, she wasn't even sure what. But she wanted it so badly, it hurt, and that made her fearless.

"Emma," he said, a warning in his tone.

"Yes, Sebastian?" she whispered, reaching up to let her finger draw an invisible design on his chest—a heart with an arrow through it. His skin was smooth as butter.

He grabbed her hand, pulling it away and holding it. "You're playing with fire, Emma," he said. His voice was soft but his tone was hard as steel. "And fire can burn."

"I've never been burned that way," she whispered. "So I'm not scared."

"Emma..."

She touched his cheek. "Yes?" she replied as her hand slid down across the cords of his neck, down to where she'd drawn the heart with the other hand, and then flattened, skimming across his skin.

His groan came from deep inside him and his eyes closed for a moment.

"Oh, Emma," he said, his voice husky with quick desire. He gathered her close and she pressed against him, savoring the hard muscles, luxuriating in the feel of him. His mouth found hers and she opened to his kiss, gasping when his tongue took over, drinking him in as though she'd been dying of thirst.

His body was so wonderful, and, in the tiny Lycra swimsuit, she could pretty much see and feel everything there was to him, all the rounded strength, all the hard edges. She ran her hand across his flesh and felt him respond. It was a power that she'd never known before—a power she wanted to test out and make her own.

This was new. This was something special, a once-in-a-lifetime thing. The air was alive around them, as though fireworks were going off on all sides. A celebration. That was what it was. A celebration of how she felt for this prince.

Because she knew, suddenly, what she'd been hiding from for days. She was in love. This was a man she could never have for her own, but she could have him for the moment. And right now, she would take what she could get.

She'd never wanted a man this way before. It was as though she were possessed, as though the needs of her body had taken over and shut off her mind in order to get their way.

He pushed aside her jersey top and exposed her breasts, touching each nipple with a gentle reverence that astonished her. The more he touched her, the more she shuddered, the aching hunger coming so strong she almost cried out.

"Oh, please, Sebastian, tell me what to do," she whispered, tangling her fingers in his hair and arching her body against his as hard as she could.

Her words stopped him cold. Rearing back, he stared at her.

"You're completely inexperienced, aren't you?" he asked, incredulous.

She shook her head, wishing she could deny it. "I'm sorry. I'll try to do it right, but tell me…"

He stared at her for a moment, and then his laughter peeled out through the cavernous area and he hugged her close.

"No, my precious Emma," he murmured, rubbing his face against hers. "We have to stop now."

"But…no, really, I want to…"

"Emma, Emma, you're priceless." He dropped quick kisses on her lips. "You're like a fresh-picked bud about to blossom into glory. I can't sully that."

"But…Sebastian, please…"

He cupped her cheek with his large hand. "I know what you want. I know exactly what you feel. I want it too. But it wouldn't be right. Not like this."

She lay back in his arms and blinked back tears. She was so happy and so sad at the same time. They weren't going to make love tonight. That meant they were never going to make love. Because as soon as morning came, they would go back to being the prince and the chef. And those two didn't mix.

"Why did you pick tonight to be such a gentleman?" she complained softly.

"Emma, I want you—probably more than I've ever wanted a woman before. But I care for you even more than that. And I'd rather protect you than use you."

She wanted to argue, but the intensity of her desire was fading now, and she knew it wasn't any use, anyway. So she stayed in his arms, curled into his embrace, because there was no place she would rather be.

She was making her way back through the darkened hallways to her bedroom an hour later. It was long past midnight. The entire castle seemed to be asleep and there wasn't a soul around. So she was surprised when the door to the second-floor library opened and Aunt Trudy stepped out directly in her path.

"Oh!" she cried, jumping half a foot into the air.

"Oh, sorry, dear. I didn't hear you coming." Trudy smiled at her. "Can't sleep? Oh, you must come with me. I have exactly the remedy for that."

Emma was glad the hall was too dark and gloomy for Trudy to see her flushed face. If she only knew what Emma had been doing with Sebastian for the last two hours, surely she wouldn't be looking so friendly.

"Come along, come along. Believe me, you'll be glad you met up with me tonight."

She led Emma back into the library. There on a large mahogany table in the center of the room was a tray with an old-fashioned-looking decanter of wine and three crystal wineglasses.

"Now you sit right down. I'm going to pour you a glass of cornberry wine. It's a traditional Meridian drink and I think you'll love it."

"Oh, good," Emma said, brightening. "I've been wanting to try it."

Trudy poured out two glasses and they toasted one another before beginning to sip.

"Wow," Emma said, gasping. "That's got a kick all right."

"Yes, it does, though one gets used to it quickly. Do you like it?"

Emma wrinkled her nose. "I'm not sure yet. I'll

have to try a little more of it before I can make my decision."

Trudy nodded. "You just take your time. It's the best remedy for sleeplessness I've ever found."

Emma took another sip, more carefully this time. "Is this what you take when you can't sleep?"

"Oh, dear, no, I don't have problems with sleep. I only sleep about four hours a night. It's been that way for years. And I get some of my best work done after midnight when there's no one around to bother me."

Emma knew that Sebastian's aunt was working on an official genealogy of the extended royal family. "I'd love to see what you've done," she said.

Trudy pursed her lips. "And you will, my dear, when I have it in condition to be seen by others. But that won't be for some time yet."

Emma emptied her glass, choking a bit but appreciative. "It's good," she said, gathering her things and preparing to take her leave. "So you think this will help me sleep?"

"Oh, definitely." She rose along with Emma, escorting her to the door. "I'll tell you a little secret. I used to give it to the king, Sebastian's father. Poor thing, once the queen died, he had horrible insomnia. I would give him a glass of cornberry wine and he would go back to his room and sleep like a baby."

Emma's ears were ringing from the strength of the drink, making her a little fuzzy, but she frowned, thinking there was something here that reminded her of something she ought to be paying attention to.

Cornberry wine. What had Tina Marie said about it? That they made it out of eikenberries now, because too many people were allergic to something in cornberries.

"Is this made out of real cornberries?" she asked Trudy.

"Oh, yes. I distill it myself at our estate in the south country. I know the wineries all use eiken-berries now, but I stick with traditions."

Emma hesitated in the doorway. "Tell me, I'm curious. How often did the king have trouble sleeping?"

"Oh, all the time. I didn't really know until the one-year anniversary of the queen's death. I found him in here, sobbing like a baby. It was such a surprise, you know, because he was always so strong and gruff. But I gave him a glass of my cornberry wine that night, and it soothed him so. Not long after, he began coming more often. Toward the end, when he was failing so badly, he came almost every night. I was so glad I was able to give him something that relieved his misery a bit."

Emma swayed, overwhelmed by what this portended. "Well," she said, her voice cracking. "Well, that's interesting. I…it never upset his stomach at all?"

"Oh, no. It's quite soothing."

"But I've heard some people can't tolerate it."

"That's right. I've heard that, too. I think that's why the national wineries started substituting other berries. But I've never had any problem with it."

"I see." Emma swallowed hard, not sure what to do. "I guess I'd better be going now. Goodnight. And…and thank you for the wine."

Her first impulse was to run to Sebastian's room with this news, if only she knew where that was. But very quickly she realized she probably shouldn't do that. Not yet. She needed to think this over. There were so many possibilities, so many ramifications. Better to go over them all before bringing this up to anyone else. After all, if this was actually what had poisoned the king, did that make Aunt Trudy a murderer? And if so, did she really want anyone else to know?

* * *

The funny thing was, when Emma got back to her room, she fell into her bed and slept like a log until morning. The cornberry wine lived up to its reputation. But that still left her with the same old dilemma. Was she going to tell Sebastian about what she suspected? The facts looked the same in the morning light as they had in the dark of night. All this cornberry-wine drinking might have had nothing to do with anything. It might all just be the work of coincidence. And she might be stirring a bee's nest of consequences she wouldn't like in the end. Maybe she ought to just keep quiet about the whole thing.

But how could she? Didn't she have to tell Sebastian? She still couldn't seem to sort it all out. She decided to wait and not do anything until she had a clear vision on this.

She helped prepare breakfast, although Chef Henri was back, and when the prince came through the kitchen she avoided his gaze, even though she knew he would think she was embarrassed about their meeting at the swimming pool. That wasn't it at all. She was feeling guilty about having information he would be interested in and not giving it to him. What was she going to do?

Louise called her at noon and she was able to tell her plans were well under way to prepare a room for her. The housekeeper had been willing, and the head maid had agreed to freshen a room very near Emma's. Louise was excited by the prospect.

"I'll book a flight right away," she said.

"Have you spoken to your parents?" Emma asked.

"What parents?" Louise said coolly. "I have heard from the adoption registry. They think they may have a lead. That's very fast, don't you think? After all these years."

A little too fast for Emma. She was hoping for a major reconciliation between her cousin and her cousin's parents before the other information came through.

Louise called back an hour later, giving her time of arrival the next day on Emma's voice mail. Meanwhile, Emma was torturing herself with indecision. She had a meeting at three with Todd to go over final plans for the coronation meal that would be distributed to the townsfolk from grills set up all over the city. But how could she keep her mind on that when all she could think about was the duchess and her cornberry wine?

She really ought to go ahead and tell Sebastian so that he could begin to try to sort it out himself.

If it were true, then he needed to know that there wasn't some murderer skulking about, ready to strike again—that there was just a dear, sweet old lady who only meant well.

"Enough!" she finally told herself. "It's got to be done. Just do it."

Throwing off her apron, she set off to find Sebastian. She searched the pool area, the libraries, the drawing rooms and parlors without success. Agatha thought he might be out at the airport with Pacio and some of the others who had a new microlight airplane they were testing out, but when she found a couple of footmen they had no idea where he was. Unfortunately, Romas overheard her asking one of them.

"Looking for the prince?" he asked, his insinuating smile just barely tolerable. "Maybe *I* can help you."

"Uh, no, thanks all the same. I really have to talk to him about something. I'll try to catch him later," she added, hoping to turn and get out of Romas' space.

But he blocked her way. "We should really get to know each other," he said, his tone suggestive. "Would you like to go for a ride? There are some great forests just north of here where the trees are already turning. Wonderful scenery. I'd love to take you out to see it."

The prospect horrified her. "Thanks, but I'm actually supposed to be working right now. I just wanted to tell Seb…the prince something. But it will keep." She gave him a bright smile. "I have to get going."

He leaned against the wall, effectively caging her in. "Not yet. We've barely begun."

"Please…"

His smile was annoyingly insinuating. "Emma, you look quite appealing when you get that worried look between your brows."

She could tell he wasn't about to move to let her pass, so she reached out to give him a push with the flat of her hand. Catching hold of her wrist, he pulled her up hard against his chest.

"I've seen you with the prince, you know. There's no future for you there. But I can show you a good time. Just give me a chance to prove it to you."

"Let me go." She was angry now, and showing it.

"One kiss, then I'll let you go."

"No!"

"Come on, Emma. You are so hot…"

He didn't get the rest of his sentence out.

Suddenly he was flailing, then choking as Sebastian had him by the neck up against the wall. Emma gasped and rubbed her wrist.

"You're asking for a well-earned lesson, Cousin," Sebastian was saying, his voice like gravel. "I'm afraid the time for it has almost come."

Romas choked until Sebastian released him, then he turned, furious, and strode off without a backward glance.

Sebastian looked at Emma. "Are you all right?"

She nodded. "He really didn't do anything, just—"

"Just acted like an idiot, as usual."

She nodded. He touched her cheek.

"Hi," he said, his eyes luminous.

"Hi," she said back, melting.

"I heard you were looking for me."

"Oh. Yes." She remembered what she had to tell him and a lot of the joy went out of the moment. "Oh, that's right. Can we go somewhere a little more private?"

"Sure." He led her into a sitting room and closed the door.

She turned to look at him. He'd evidently just come in from a business meeting of some sort as he was wearing a silk suit that fitted him like a glove. He'd unbuttoned his collar and pulled his tie loose and to one side, giving him a casual, devil-may-care look, and she thought she'd never seen a more attractive man.

"Sebastian, did your father have allergies?" she asked, getting right to the point.

"Allergies?" He frowned, thinking for a moment. "Not that I remember. Why?"

"Because…I think you ought to ask the specialist in Zurich to test for whatever it is in cornberries that makes people react."

"Cornberries?" He was looking skeptical. "I know some people do have reactions to cornberries, but I don't think you can die from it."

She shook her head. "I think you ought to research that. Find out for sure."

He searched her eyes. "Emma, this isn't just a guess on your part. It's coming from something specific, isn't it? What is it?"

Closing her eyes, she took a deep breath and told him about her midnight visit with his aunt and what she'd told her.

"That can't be it," he said, frowning. "Can it?"

"I hope not. I know the duchess wouldn't have dreamed of giving your father anything that would harm him. But I think you'd better investigate."

He drummed his fingers on the back of a chair for a moment, thinking. "It does fit the time frame." He looked at her again. "Oh, my God, Emma. What if it's true?" His gaze was haunted. "My poor father. My poor aunt."

She nodded sadly, her eyes stinging. She was sorry to lay this on him, but it was best that he know.

He hesitated, looking at her. "You know, it's interesting what she told you about my father being so affected by my mother's death. I never knew that. I'm glad you told me."

She wanted to take his hand in hers but she held back the impulse. "I'd better get back," she said. "We're pretty busy preparing for the ball tomorrow."

"Ah, yes." He grimaced. "One more ordeal of that sort to get through."

"An ordeal?" she echoed, half chuckling. "I'm sure it pains you to have all those beautiful women throwing themselves at you. Poor baby."

Listening to her cynical tone, he grinned.

"Well, I'll admit it's not quite pistols at forty paces, but I can think of better ways to spend my evening."

She shrugged. "Then you should go ahead and pick one of them as your future wife. The others will have to stop bothering you like this."

He grimaced. "You know, the great thing about this ball situation is that I don't have to go into it worrying about whether or not the woman I choose loves me for myself or for my position. It's obvious. If she's here, she's a 'position' gal. I don't have to agonize, I know exactly where she stands."

Emma nodded. "There is that, I suppose," she allowed, wondering why they were still on this subject. It wasn't exactly a favorite of hers. "Where do they get these women, anyway? Duchess Trudy said that they aren't all royal."

"They may not be royal themselves, but they all have ties to the ruling fraternity—European royalty or the American governing class or South American ex-dictators. The field I'm supposed to choose from is not as wide open as it might seem."

"But the women are all beautiful."

He considered, raising one eyebrow. "Well, at least semi-beautiful," he corrected. "And definitely wealthy. Believe me, our minister of finance has been over the financial backgrounds of every one of these women. If a woman can bring a little money into the bargain, so much the better."

"Good luck, then," she said, turning abruptly.

She'd had all she could take of thinking about Sebastian marrying one of the rich lovelies.

Well, there you go, Emma thought to herself a few minutes later as she hurried back to the kitchen. *Beauty and money. That's what they want. And I don't have either one.*

Luckily there was a lot of work to do and she wasn't going to have time to obsess about Sebastian and his many eager women. But at least she'd given him a new lead in the poisoning mystery. It was probably best to lay that to rest, even if it did mean implicating Duchess Trudy.

CHAPTER ELEVEN

Louise arrived bright and early the next morning. Emma went down to help her with bags and show her to her room.

"I know you're going to enjoy it here," she said.

"Oh, yes, I'm sure of it. It's beautiful. And, anyway, I have plans."

"Plans?" Emma wasn't sure she liked the sound of that.

"Yes. And I've already contacted Agatha. She's been a big help."

Emma stopped in the middle of the corridor and stared at her.

"What? How did you already meet Agatha? You just got here."

Louise waved a hand in the air. "You know me; I have contacts everywhere. I know someone who went to school with Agatha and I asked her to introduce us. We've been corresponding by e-mail for days now."

"How many days?" Emma asked suspiciously.

"Well, two. But we're in accord about you."

"About me?" she cried in dismay. There was nothing worse than knowing friends were discussing you among themselves.

"Yes." Louise gave her an impish smile. "We're going to work on giving you a makeover."

Emma glared at her cousin. "I don't wear makeup."

"Emma Valentine, it's about time you did."

Louise was a very persuasive person. Emma knew, one way or another, she was going to end up in makeup. And she knew she was going to hate it.

It was even worse later that afternoon when she took a break from counting out silverware in preparation for the dinner before that evening's ball, and went up to see if Louise needed anything. What she found was what looked like a rummage sale going on in her room. Louise and Agatha had gotten very chummy very quickly. It turned out the threatened makeover was the cause of their bonding.

"We're going through your clothes," Louise told a horrified Emma. "This is a *What Not to Wear* moment. We're trying to figure out what your style should be. You've never really settled on one, you know."

"Sure I have," Emma said defensively. "Tomboy Retro, I call it. Fits me to a *t*."

Agatha frowned, looking at her speculatively. "You may call it Tomboy Retro," she said. "I'd call it sexually neutral ambiguity."

"Or aggressively ambivalent teenager," Louise offered up.

Emma looked at them both in exasperation. "Do you know how annoying it is to have people tell you how to dress?"

Louise shrugged. "You know what they say— you've got to break a few eggs to make an omelet."

Agatha nodded her agreement. "Great advances in civilization only happen through trial and error. And a lot of strife."

"We've got a great idea," Louise said happily. "Let's do the makeover tonight."

Emma winced. "Why tonight?"

"Why not? It's the perfect time. You said Chef Henri was handling the buffet dinner for the ball. You'll have nothing to do once the dinner has been served and the dancing begins. There are three women not invited to the ball—you, me, and Agatha. Let's have a party of our own."

"And *I'm* supposed to be the entertainment?"

"Who better?"

Agatha grinned. "We're going to dress you up like a Barbie doll."

"Oh," Emma cried, appalled. "How wonderful."

"You wait. It'll be fun."

Emma tried to look fierce, but they were acting so silly, she was actually having a hard time not laughing. "You two are full of it, you know."

"Come on. This is so much fun."

"Okay. You just go on having fun." She stuck her nose in the air in mock superiority. "I've got more important things to do."

Important things like beating egg whites to stiff peaks and working on the perfect veal reduction. But they were exactly the things that she loved doing, so she was actually in her element, even if she was missing all the brutal opinions on her dressing habits going on up in her room.

Sebastian came into the kitchen to talk to Chef Henri just before the guests were to begin arriving. She had to admit, he looked even better in his white royal uniform with its gold braid and epaulettes than he had in the Italian suit. He was, in fact, to die for, and she had a hard time catching her breath again after he gave her a wink.

He *did* like her. She couldn't deny that. And that knowledge warmed her for a while. But once the beautiful women in their fabulous ball gowns began arriving, her mood darkened. She was jealous. No point trying to hide it.

The local newspaper had a spread giving odds on various women and how they seemed to be doing in the competition for Sebastian's hand in marriage.

"As if they know anything at all," Aunt Trudy had said. "They make this claptrap up out of thin air."

"They make most of what they write about up out of thin air," Agatha agreed. She was down in the kitchen on one of her regularly timed expeditions for snacks. "Haven't you ever noticed that they are wrong more than they're right?"

Emma just shook her head. How could these people stand it, being written about this way, day in and day out? She was so glad she was never going to have to deal with that again once she left Meridia.

"Pay it no mind," Aunt Trudy said.

But how could she not? The kitchen staff was giggling over it all afternoon, until Emma thought she would go mad. She'd even taken a look at the article herself, and, she had to admit, the women the newspapers had featured were accomplished, exciting women. Damn them all!

She was making a last-minute inspection of the table settings when she overheard a pair of them waiting to go down the reception line.

"And as to who is going to end up as Queen of Meridia, well, I've been told I'm definitely a front-runner," a flaming-haired temptress in a skintight gown that showed off her voluptuous figure was saying.

"How so?" responded her friend.

"Supposedly the prince likes me best. Haven't you noticed how he looks at me?"

The friend bristled. "Oh, sure. And you can see that he's thinking, *How did she manage to squeeze that big old body into that little bitty dress?*"

"Oh, very funny, Renee. He told me I could have the first dance with him tonight."

"We'll see who gets the last dance," Renee retorted. "That will tell the tale."

They wandered off and Emma sighed. If Sebastian picked one of those women... But what did it matter? It was none of her concern.

The next hour or so went quickly. The kitchen was busy tonight. And then, she could hear the musicians tuning up in the ballroom, and she excused herself. She couldn't bear to stay in the kitchen, hearing the music and knowing Sebastian was dancing with one woman after another, holding each in his arms in a way he would never hold her.

Still, she returned to her room with a sort of dread not knowing what Agatha and Louise had been cooking up while she was gone. At least being with them would give her something else to think about.

Opening the door, she was surprised to find everything neat and orderly again. Her two friends sat on her bed just finishing up their dinners, which they had taken on trays.

"You're here already?" Louise cried. "Oh, great. We'll get right to it."

"Do we have to?" she said, groaning.

"Yes, we have to. You don't get offers like this every day, Emma. You're lucky."

"Come on," Agatha chimed in. "This is going to be fun."

And it was.

Despite everything, she had to admit it. She washed her hair and Agatha got busy giving her a trim and blow-drying it, while Louise began work on her makeup, explaining all about foundations and highlighting and all sorts of things Emma had never paid any attention to before.

"As a card-carrying member of twenty-first

century womanhood, you're supposed to know these things," Louise chided.

She listened intently. She would learn about this the same way she learned about everything. But that didn't mean she'd ever use the knowledge.

The makeup took almost two hours. Not that Louise was working on it the whole time. They spent most of their time talking and joking and taking snack breaks now and then. Agatha gave her a manicure and she marveled at how pretty her hands looked with the shiny pink polish.

As for the makeup—she wasn't allowed to look in a mirror, so she had no idea how that was going.

Finally, Louise and Agatha glanced at each other and nodded.

"Okay," Louise said. "Take a look."

Emma got up gingerly. Her face felt strange and she was afraid to smile for fear of cracking something. Creeping up to her mirror, she closed her eyes until she was in front of it, then opened them again.

"Oh, no!" she cried, her eyes tragic. "Oh, it's horrible."

"No, no!" Louise said. "You're just not used to it."

"I look like a clown." Emma grabbed a damp towel and began rubbing her face vigorously, while the two others shrieked and ran to stop her. They were too late. She'd wiped her face clean, destroying two hours of work.

"I would die before I would go in public like that," she said firmly. "Face it, ladies. I'm just not the type for makeup."

"Oh." Louise looked crushed.

But Agatha had a thought. "You know, she's right," she said, her head to the side as she looked at Emma. "She's not really the type for heavy makeup. But I'll bet something that just hints at it would do very well on her. You ought to try something with a bit more subtlety."

"Good idea," Louise said, watching Emma's reaction anxiously. "I'll do it again, only much better. Please, Emma," she added as Emma shook her head. "This time, I promise, you're going to like it."

Emma hesitated. She had no faith in this at all, but she hated to disappoint her cousin. "All right," she said at last. "You have exactly fifteen minutes."

"Then what's going to happen?"

"I'm going to bed. I've been working all day. I'm tired."

The two young women exchanged glances again.

"Okay, okay, fifteen minutes," Louise said. "Just give me room."

She worked quickly, not wasting any time on chitchat. And when the fifteen minutes were up, she stood back and let Agatha work a little more magic with the hairstyle.

"Now take a look."

Emma had little hope this time, but she was surprised by what she saw. She looked harder at her face in the mirror. A little light blush, a bit of eyeliner, some mascara and eye shadow, a touch of pink lipstick, a cuter-than-heck hairstyle, and she was a different woman.

"Wow. Is that really me? I like this. This looks good." She fluffed her hair a little. "I look…pretty." She looked at the other two in wonder.

Agatha gave a gurgling laugh. "You've always been pretty. Now you look pulled together. Like you're a grown-up woman and know what you're doing."

"Right," Louise said. "Now for the clothes."

Emma bit her tongue and held back what she really wanted to say. They were so excited about this, and they'd done such good work, she decided to let them have their way—no matter how annoying that was. They tried a couple of Louise's outfits that didn't quite do it, then a long, slinky silk dress from Agatha's closet, and that was the one they all agreed fitted the bill.

"You look spectacular," Louise said, her eyes shining, and no one disagreed.

The dress was cut low, showing off more cleavage than Emma had known she had, and fitted her form to perfection. The pastel rainbow colors of the fabric seemed to change in the lamplight as she moved.

"Let's go take pictures."

Emma had forgotten that she'd promised to go down to the room especially set up for picture-taking on the first floor.

"Do we really have to do this?"

"You know, Emma," Louise said, "it would really be a help to me if you would let me take some pictures. I'm casting about on what I'm going to do with my life and it has occurred to me that I might change careers and go into business doing personal makeovers for a living."

"What?" That was the first she'd heard of this new scheme.

"You don't think I did a nice job on you?"

Louise looked innocent as a newborn babe but Emma sensed something fishy going on.

"I didn't say that. I think you did a wonderful job on me. I love what you did—the second time, anyway."

"Well, so do I. So let's go downstairs. I just want to take some pictures in case I start working up a portfolio."

Emma sighed. "Okay. But I'm not going anywhere near the ballroom."

"The ballroom?" Louise repeated, her eyes huge and guileless. "Oh, the ballroom."

"You don't want to just slip by the ballroom and take a little peek?" Agatha asked wistfully.

"No," Emma said firmly. "I am not going anywhere near that ballroom."

They took the elevator down, laughing like teenagers, and made their way to the picture room. They spent the next half-hour taking pictures of each other. The music from the ballroom was a constant backdrop.

"Just one more of Emma," Agatha said at last. "I want a formal pose, so stand over here with your back to these double doors. They'll really frame you nicely."

Emma did as she was asked and Louise started telling a story that was making her laugh so hard she didn't notice at first that, instead of taking a picture, Agatha had left the room.

"Just stand where you are," Louise said when Agatha's absence came up. "She's about to take a picture."

"I'm beginning to feel like I'm getting my teeth X-rayed," Emma grumbled. "Isn't that when they usually leave the room?"

A sound from behind made her turn. The double doors were swinging open and there was Agatha. But Agatha quickly stepped out of the way and then…then there was Prince Sebastian.

She stared at him. He stared at her. His gaze was so full of affection and admiration, she couldn't look away. It was intoxicating and her head was feeling as though it had just been filled with champagne bubbles.

She didn't know where to turn. The double doors had opened onto a short hallway that led right into the ballroom, and most of the guests were looking in at her. She wanted to run, and yet she couldn't. He was there. She could never run from him.

"Emma, Emma," he said softly, his eyes glowing in the lamplight. "You look more beautiful than ever."

Because he'd said it, because his eyes said it, she believed it. For the first time in her life, she felt beautiful.

"May I have this dance?" he asked, holding out his arm.

She walked toward him as though compelled to. He led her into the ballroom and as his arms came around her he whispered in her ear, "It's the last dance."

She gasped. She knew what that meant, but...

"Can you do a Viennese Waltz?" he asked as the music started.

"I've never done one," she said.

"You're going to do one now. Just relax and let me lead you."

The music grew, swelling to fill the room, and they began to whirl around and around. She was nervous at first, not sure she could keep up, but his strong arms kept her going and soon the steps were automatic.

And that was when what was merely amusing became magic. They were floating in the stars, turned and swirling, held up by the wonderful Strauss music. She'd never experienced anything like it, and when the music slowed she clung to Sebastian, wishing it could start up all over again.

Sebastian signaled the orchestra leader and the music didn't stop after all. Instead, they began to play "It Had To Be You" and Sebastian looked down into her eyes as they began to sway together. Then he pulled her closer and began to sing softly along with the orchestra, into her ear.

She closed her eyes. This had to be a dream.

But all good things had to end at last, and the music finally stopped. They stopped as well, but he still held her. She tilted her head up to look at him, and he leaned down and kissed her on her lips.

And then he turned back to the others.

But Emma was still in the dream.

"Hey, it's after midnight, Cinderella," Agatha whispered, tugging on her arm. "This way to your pumpkin."

She let Agatha lead her but she was floating. Sebastian's arms were still around her and…

"Come on," Louise told the other two happily. "I snagged some stuff from the dessert buffet. Let's go up and have a feast."

Emma looked at her blankly. She still had his voice in her ear, still had his wonderful scent in her head, still felt his breath on her cheek. She wanted to close her eyes and hold all those things close for ever.

Louise frowned. "Are you okay? Do you hate us?"

It took her a moment to understand what Louise had said. She shook her head. "Why would I hate you?" she asked, then slowly she began to sink back to earth. "Oh, you mean because you two tricked me into dancing with Sebastian? I could never hate you for that."

But she sighed as they made their way back to the room. He'd danced the last dance with her, but it didn't mean a thing. She knew better than to expect anything to come of it. Still, she would have that memory for the rest of her life.

Seeing her face, Louise gave her a hug.

"Things will work out for the best," she said sympathetically. "Generally, they do in the end."

The next morning started out with a jolt. Louise came bursting into her room before she'd come fully awake, thrilled by a call from the adoption registry.

"This is so exciting. They've found my birth mother, and guess what? I've got a sister in Australia. Her name is Jodie Simpson. Can you believe it? A whole new family to deal with."

Emma blinked sleepily and tried not to yawn. "I wish you luck. But don't forget your old family. We love you, too."

"I know that." Louise hugged her. "You've been so good to me. Thanks for letting me come here to lick my wounds and heal a little."

"Louise, call your parents. Please? You know they're heartbroken right now."

Louise squeezed her hand but didn't respond. Instead she prattled on about Australia. "I'm going to have to go back to the UK right away. They want me to see some documents."

"All right. I'm glad you came."

"Me too."

As she flitted back out again Emma wondered how long it would be before she saw her cousin again. Somehow all her relationships seemed to be in a strange state of flux these days.

A bit later she headed down to the kitchen, full of trepidation. She knew something bad was bound to happen. And sure enough, the first thing she saw was the local paper scattered across the kitchen table. This time the headline read, PRINCE COMPLIMENTS CHEF—AGAIN! And there was a picture of Emma floating in Sebastian's arms in the ballroom.

She hated that the picture was there for everyone to see. She hated that anyone had seen the two of them at the time. She hated everything that tried to make the way she felt about the prince seem cheap and tawdry. If only he weren't a prince and they were all alone in some strange city where neither of them knew anyone else…

But there wasn't much point in dreaming things like that. Reality might not be so pretty but it was here to stay.

There was yelling in the breakfast room again. She thought she knew what the problem was. Though she hadn't noticed it at the time—actually, she hadn't noticed anything but Sebastian at the time—she now realized that the faces around the ballroom watching them hadn't been happy ones. No one had been pleased that she'd been the prince's choice for the last dance. She debated going into the breakfast room and confronting them all, but thought better of it.

A few moments later, Sebastian emerged looking somewhat annoyed.

Her heart lurched and memories of the night before swept over her so strongly, she had to put out a hand to steady herself. And then she realized he was coming straight toward her.

"Good morning," he said, smiling at her right in front of everyone in the kitchen. "I need to talk to you. Let's go to the library."

"But…" She looked back at the breakfast room.

"Let them yell themselves hoarse. I'm not going to change my mind."

She looked at him speculatively. He looked a

little angry over the criticism from his ministers, but, on the whole, rather pleased with himself.

"What are they angry about?" she asked, walking along beside him. "Because you danced with me last night?"

"That's only part of it. They're also going hysterical because I told them I had a new condition that had to be met before I would agree to take the crown."

They stopped in front of the library and he took her hands, smiling down at her.

"What is your new condition?" Emma asked, suddenly dreading what he was going to say. "Unless it's none of my business."

"It's very much your business." He touched her cheek. "I told them I would only stay if you agreed to marry me and stay as well."

Her world tilted on its axis. She had to reach a hand out against the wall to steady herself again.

"What?"

"You're the one who reminded me that I had the upper hand in these negotiations. And I decided to use my advantage." He stood holding her hands, looking proud of himself.

"I see." Though she didn't. She was still stunned and unsure what all this meant.

"So what do you think?" He raised an eyebrow

and looked so darn sure of himself. "Are you going to like being queen?"

Her mind was like a lost rowboat in a stormy sea. She was only vaguely clear on what he'd done. But she did know she didn't like the way he was doing this.

Did he really want her to marry him? Or had he merely used that threat as a weapon in a fight with his ministers? It was a little hard to tell which it might be.

"I don't understand," she said, shaking her head.

"It's simple. They wanted you gone. I said, no, in fact, you would be here for a very long time and you would be here as my wife. A couple of them went hysterical, claiming they would never stand for it. I told them I was out of here unless they okayed our marriage. And there you have it."

He obviously thought she should be shouting with joy. Here he'd faced them all in her name. But this reminded her more of their first clash, when he'd commandeered her to sew on his braid. He seemed to think he could just run right over people and always get his way. Well, he had another think coming.

"You know, Sebastian, you might have spoken to me about it before you told the world."

His brows drew together and his eyes darkened. "What are you saying? That you don't want to marry me?"

What she really wanted was to throttle him.

"No," she said aloud, speaking precisely, "as a matter of fact, I don't."

He looked incredulous, but there was no more time to talk. A couple of the men he'd been arguing with had found them and seemed ready to continue the fight.

"Look, you'd better think it over," he said, effectively dismissing her in order to rejoin them. "I'll talk to you later."

He turned toward the men and she got away as quickly as she could. Her heart was beating so hard, she was afraid she might have a heart attack. Extreme emotions cascaded through her in a jumble that was hard to untangle—elation, anger, pride, resentment, bitterness, disappointment. They were all there. But they weren't pleasant.

"Hello there, pretty lady."

She whirled, only to find Sebastian's cousin had followed her out.

"Oh, Romas."

"Don't start backing away from me. I'm not going to hit on you this time. Sebastian has staked you out as his and that's good enough for me. My only question is, is it good enough for you?"

"What are you talking about?"

"You know very well that our boy, Sebastian, has been a major player all his life. How do you know you're not just his latest whim?"

She stared at him, wishing she had a good response, but the hollow feeling in the pit of her stomach was all she had. She turned away and left him.

"Have a nice day," he called after her, chuckling.

She shook her head.

But Romas was the least of her problems. She was so angry with Sebastian. He was being so high-handed and making vast assumptions. He seemed to take for granted that she wanted exactly what he wanted. How had he got that idea?

And did he really think she was going to drop her career, just like that? Did all the goals she had met, all the honors she'd received, mean so little in his eyes? Maybe he didn't understand how focussed she'd been on her career, how she'd pushed aside all the fun and crazy things most people did in their twenties to concentrate on constant work in order to get good enough to reach the top levels. And now she was supposed to throw all that away and become…what? A sort of royal hostess person?

And, worst of all, nowhere had she heard the words, *I love you.*

An hour later, she was in a castle car being driven by Pacio, the footman. She was going back to London, at least for a day or two. She had to get away to someplace where she could think without Sebastian around to distract her. She needed distance. She needed to do something to stop her head from spinning like a top.

"Where are we going?" she said, leaning forward and looking out the window. "This doesn't look like the way to the airport."

"Tina Marie wants to see you," Pacio replied. "She heard you were leaving and she asked me to take you by."

"I've got a plane to catch."

"We'll make it. You've got plenty of time."

Her mind was racing with the things Sebastian had said and she didn't really have room for worrying about why Tina Marie might want to see her, so she didn't ask any more questions.

A few minutes later, she was climbing the stairs to Tina Marie's place. The older woman greeted her like a long-lost child. She made her come in and sit down and have some sweet, thick coffee, chattering all the while. Then she brought out a scrapbook and a stack of papers.

"I've been looking for this for a week and I've finally found it. I asked Pacio to bring you here because I want to show this to you."

"What is that?"

"An old scrapbook I used to keep when I was working at the castle. I kept newspaper clippings in here. And I wanted you to see this one."

She pulled out a clipping turned dark brown with age. "I know how terrible you felt when you served the unicomus at dinner the other night."

Emma groaned. "Oh, don't remind me. That was the worst night of my life."

"I know. You thought you had let everyone down, especially Prince Sebastian. But you know what? It's happened before. Look."

She held out the clipping. Emma squinted at it, trying without much success to make out the picture on the darkened paper.

"Oh, it's a fish on a platter. A unicomus?" She looked at Tina Marie, who was nodding.

"See the headline?"

Emma read it out loud. "Queen in Fish Faux Pas".

"You see? Queen Marguerite made the same

mistake you did. She was from Italy and thought the unicomus a delicacy, so she ordered her cook to prepare it for a special dinner. The kitchen staff at that time didn't help her out any more than yours did."

"Oh, poor thing. Was she crushed?"

"She wept for two days, and the king didn't help matters, going around like a grouchy bear the whole time." Tina Marie shook her head, remembering. "But you know? In the end it was for the best, because the queen came to a turning point. Two days of weeping, and then she began to realize, it was just a silly fish, after all. Why was everyone making such a big deal out of a silly mistake about a fish?"

Tina Marie shook her finger at Emma. "That was the day the worm turned. She began to realize her life would be as good or as bad as she made it herself. She couldn't depend on others to make her happiness for her. It took time for her to come to her full strength as a woman and a queen, but she began the process that day."

Emma began looking through the scrapbook. It was a treasure trove of Meridian history. Before long, Tina Marie had told Pacio to go back to the castle and she'd started to fix up a bed where

Emma could get some sleep. The plane reservations for London were long forgotten.

Emma took a refreshing nap, had some delicious soup, and then sat up late listening to Tina Marie's stories and telling a few of her own. By morning, she felt a good deal calmer about things.

She'd called her brother Max the evening before, just to see how things were going at the Bella Lucia.

"Oh, don't worry about us," he assured her. "We're doing well."

"Really? How's Mary Beth working out?"

"Fine. She doesn't have your flair as yet, but she's working on it. A little more seasoning and she'll be a fine chef."

For some reason, that didn't seem to be what she'd wanted to hear, and she wasn't exactly sure why.

"I'll be back soon."

He hesitated. "I don't know, Emma. We'd love to have you back, of course, but I thought that once you were out on your own you would see that it's way past time for you to spread your wings and do something bigger. You need to get out from under Dad's influence and find yourself out there in the world."

His statement had surprised her, but she knew

he was right. Bella Lucia was a part of her past now. She could go back. She could work at the restaurant again, spending her days doing what she'd been doing for years. But did she really want to? She would never see Sebastian again if she did.

Funny—when she put those two things together and compared them—the thought of never going back to the restaurant and the thought of never going back to Sebastian—it was pretty obvious which prospect would break her heart.

And she would miss Meridia, and Tina Marie and Aunt Trudy and Agatha and Merik—how quickly they had all become a part of her life.

At the very least, she had to fulfill her commitment to the coronation. She couldn't leave that to other people. Wasn't she always telling Sebastian that responsibilities had to be addressed? Civilization itself would come unraveled if no one picked up the thread of his responsibility.

A long walk had helped her put things into perspective, so she wasn't shocked to find Sebastian waiting to see her when she got back.

Her heart leaped at the sight of him. No matter what, she couldn't stop herself from loving him.

He looked serious and even a bit worried. He had a picnic basket with him and a CD player and a huge bouquet of yellow flowers. He asked if she would go up to the watch meadow with him, back to where they'd picnicked before.

She only hesitated for a few seconds and Tina Marie's secret wink helped her make up her mind.

"I'd love to go with you," she said, and the look of relief on his face was as good as gold in terms of a reward.

They climbed the hill and spread out a blanket. When she opened the basket, she found a bottle of champagne and two glasses. Were they for refreshment or celebration? She didn't know, so she left them where they were.

Looking at Sebastian again, she noticed his lip was swollen. And then she realized he had a large purple circle under one eye. How had she missed that?

"What happened?" she cried.

He touched his lip and winced. "I finally had it out with Romas."

"Oh, no. What did you do?"

"We were very civilized about it, actually." He sat down next to her on the blanket. "We used boxing gloves and had an umpire. And I beat the tar out of him."

She hid her smile. "It looks like he got in a shot or two himself."

"Mere flesh wounds."

She shook her head. "Those flesh wounds are going to look pretty spectacular at your coronation."

He turned to look into her eyes, searching them. "Is there going to be a coronation?" he asked softly.

She turned away. "You can't put it all on my shoulders like this."

"Why not? You put it all on mine."

He was right, she supposed. She deserved his reply.

"But before we go any further, I thought you would want to know… It looks like the cornberries were the culprit in my father's death. He had heart disease, but the reaction to the berries probably made things worse."

She bit her lip, nodding. "I'm sorry, Sebastian." She squeezed his hand, wishing there were words that actually helped when people were in pain. Then she remembered. "But what about Aunt Trudy?"

He shook his head, his eyes hooded. "I'm not going to tell her. There's no point. But I am going to make sure she doesn't go on offering people cornberry wine."

"Good." It was a relief that Trudy wouldn't be

told. What heartbreak it would have been for her. Emma loved Sebastian even more for being sensitive to that.

"Now how about some of the wine I brought?" he said.

She nodded and pulled the bottle out of the basket, looking for the bottle opener. Meanwhile, he put a romantic CD into the player and turned it on.

"What are you doing?" she asked, laughing at him.

He leaned back and looked at her. "I spent a sleepless night trying to figure out what I did wrong yesterday," he told her. "I even asked my sister, much as I hated to do it. I got an earful about a lot of things, but most of all, I've been told I'm not romantic enough. So I'm giving it a try."

"Interesting." She had to work hard to keep her smile under control.

"Isn't it?" He opened the bottle and poured the golden liquid out into the glasses. Handing her one, he raised his in a toast.

"To romance," he said. "To sunny days and kisses in the rain and daisy chains."

"Hear hear," she said, clinking glasses with him. His lack of romance was only a part of what had bothered her the day before. But he was certainly trying. She had to hand it to him on that.

He glanced at his watch and looked out into the sky as though he was expecting something to happen. She tried to look where he was looking to get some idea of what was bothering him, but she didn't have a clue.

"How am I doing so far?" he asked her.

"Pretty good," she told him, purposely staying a bit low-key for now. "Keep it up."

"Okay." He gritted his teeth. "Ah, hell. Listen, you like Meridia, don't you?"

"It's a wonderful country."

"And you care about its future."

"Of course."

"And you're interested in its past."

"Yes."

He threw his hands out. "So what the hell's the problem?"

"Oh, Sebastian."

"Okay. I'm sorry." He grimaced, realizing he'd strayed off the beaten path for a moment there. "Okay." He licked his lips. "I suppose you wonder what life will be like if you become queen."

She blinked at him. "Not really."

"Well, I'm going to tell you anyway. Here it is. Your life will be what you want to make of it. I know you have a career. You're a top chef, one of the best. You don't have to give that up. In fact, you'll have resources you could never have on your own. You told me you wanted to write cookbooks and be on TV shows. As queen, you'll have television networks and book publishers yapping about your heels like pet poodles. You'll be able to do whatever you want. You can teach in cooking seminars. You can set up a college of Epicurean wisdom if you want."

She cocked her head to the side, considering. "That all sounds pretty good."

"It does, doesn't it?" He looked pleased. "But I've got to be honest. That's not all. The most important thing, the bottom line—your main duty as queen will be to have my children. Think you can handle that?" He gazed at her levelly.

She colored. "I don't know. I don't know if I have any talent in that direction."

His smile was crooked and his eyes sparkled. "Don't worry. I recognize raw talent when I see it. We're going to hone your skills."

She was beginning to feel a little giddy. "You sound like you're trying to sell me options on a new life."

"In a way, that's exactly what I'm doing."

"But, Sebastian, you don't have to sell me

anything. I understand all that. And I know you are a wonderful man."

He frowned. "Then what's the hold-up?"

She closed her eyes and groaned.

"I know. It's that same old 'If you don't know I can't tell you' again. Right?"

He looked so bemused by it all, she had to laugh. "Sort of," she admitted.

He sobered, taking her hand in his and lacing fingers.

"The truth is, I do love this country and I do want it to succeed. And I do want to be their leader. But I'm not sure I can do a good job of it without you. There's something strong and pure and good in you, Emma. I need it in my life. I need someone to tell me when I'm running rough-shod over other people. I need someone to see when I'm about to go off the rails for whatever reason, someone I can trust to set me right again." He looked deep into her eyes. "Can you be that person?"

She thought for a moment, frowning. "What if I were to say I would only marry you if you pledged *not* to take the crown? What would you say then?"

"Emma, are you kidding? I'm not just trying to hire you as a sort of assistant king to help me run the country. Marrying you is number one. Being with you is all I need. Say the word and we'll be gone tomorrow. I've got a yacht waiting for me in the Caribbean. I think you'll love sailing."

"Save it for a vacation," she said. A good, warm feeling was growing inside her. She was beginning to think this relationship might have a chance after all.

"That wasn't really a very good test," Sebastian was saying, "because I know you. And I know you want me to accept the crown. But when we marry, I'll pledge my life to you as well as my heart. And if there comes a time when you feel you can't take it here any longer, all you have to do is say the word, and we'll find someone else to take over."

She nodded happily. She was beginning to believe him.

He was glancing at his watch again and looking around at the sky.

"Where is that damn…?"

"What are you looking for?"

"Oh, nothing."

The sound of an engine finally came through the trees and he swung back to look. "There it is!" he cried, pointing toward the gap between the stands of forest. "Here he comes. Look."

She looked. A small microlight plane was coming into the clearing ahead. It seemed to be pulling a long banner behind it, but the banner was tangled and she couldn't read what it said.

"See that little plane?" Sebastian said, grinning. "It's Pacio."

"Oh, how cute. Pacio is a man of many talents."

"Let's hope so," Sebastian was muttering, beginning to look worried.

She frowned. The plane was sputtering. "But wait. Doesn't the engine sound a little funny?"

"It sure does. Oh, my God, he's going to crash!"

They both jumped up and began running toward the clearing.

The little plane had landed in a tree and was sputtering, then the engine quit entirely and the plane slid down through the trees, onto the ground. It hit with a thump rather than a smash-up, and as they approached they could see Pacio climbing out of the wreckage and waving to them.

"Thank God," Sebastian said. "It looks like he's okay."

"Oh. Look."

Emma pointed up at the top of the tree where the banner had been ripped from its moorings on the plane. It now spread out across the tree, showing everything, which included the royal crest and the wording, "Emma, I love you" in huge letters.

She stared at it for a long moment, then turned and looked at Sebastian. "Did you do that?" she asked softly.

He nodded, looking wary. "Too over the top?" he asked uncertainly. "Too public? Maybe I should have done it in code."

She was shaking her head. "No," she said. "No, it's just right." And she threw herself into his arms, raising her face for his kisses. "Oh, Sebastian," she sighed. "You're so crazy."

"Crazy in love with you," he corrected, nuzzling her ear. "Emma, Emma, I need you to marry me."

He kissed her cheeks and then her eyelids and then her nose, and finally her lips.

"It was only last week that you and I talked about love right here on this hillside," he reminded her softly. "Neither one of us was sure that such a thing existed. A lot can change in a week."

"Yes."

"So tell me, Emma. Do you believe in love?"

"Oh, yes."

"And will you marry me?"

Before she could answer, shouts could be heard. They looked down and saw a crowd coming up from where the plane had landed. They were carrying Pacio on their shoulders.

"People are coming up the hill," Sebastian said. "You'd better decide quickly. They've seen the banner. When they get here, they'll want answers."

She shook her head. "Is this the way it's going to be? 'The people' will rule our lives?"

He nodded, smiling down at her. "That's what you're signing up for. If you marry me."

She sighed. "Okay, then. I may be crazy myself, because the answer is 'yes'. I love you and I'd love to marry you."

He gave a whoop, swung her up into his arms and kissed her, hard. The crowd coming up the hill began to cheer and the sun broke out through the clouds.

"You see?" he told her, still holding her high. "The world looks better already."

She nodded, tears beginning to overflow and stream down her face.

This was going to be the beginning of a real happily-ever-after life. It had to be.

EPILOGUE

HISTORY BEING MADE.

That phrase kept pounding in his head as Sebastian prepared for the coronation. History was being made and he was a part of it. An epic or a tragedy? Time would tell.

A horse-drawn carriage was taking him toward the cathedral where the ceremony would take place. He looked out on the land he loved, gleaming in the sunlight. His heart swelled.

And then he looked out at the people. They lined the road, four or five deep in some places. There was an eerie silence about them, though a murmur seemed to follow him as he passed. Most faces weren't hostile, exactly, just curious. As Emma kept reminding him, all they knew about him was what they read in the papers. Would he be able to prove himself to them?

"Yes."

He said it aloud, firmly. And he believed it.

The cathedral shimmered like silver ahead. The carriage came to a stop and the honor guard stood at attention to escort him up the wide stone stairs. At the top he stopped and turned, slowly surveying the crowd. Here and there a banner waved. "Phony King" said one. "Bring back Prince Julius" said another. A third was obscene, but it almost made him laugh, and the first thing he thought was, he had to remember it for Emma.

Emma. He wished they could have married first, so that she could be beside him today. Then the banners could have read, "Phony King + Traitor Chef". That almost made him laugh again, and he turned to go into the cathedral.

An hour of time-honored ritual made an important impression on them all. This was real and it was serious—a culmination of what generations of Meridians had built in this lakeside land. Strangely, the more the pomp and circumstances swelled, the more humble he felt.

He caught sight of Emma standing at the back of the cathedral, dressed in a beautiful silk dress that flowed around her regally, though he knew she was about to dash back to the castle and don her chef whites. Their eyes met as he passed her. Hers shimmered with unshed tears. Watching him take the crown had obviously been emotional for her.

Coming out onto the stone terrace, he was almost surprised to see that the crowds were still there, waiting to see him again. Custom would have him going straight back into the carriage and riding to the castle. Somehow, that didn't fit with the way he was feeling. Motioning to his honour guard to pause, he went to the edge of the terrace and saluted the crowd.

A murmur simmered and someone yelled, "Hey, King!"

King. He smiled. One of the honor guards, an old timer, came up and whispered a warning in his ear.

"Some of 'em's got rotten fruit," he told him. "Don't stay still too long. They'll start throwin' things."

Looking out, he knew the old man was right. But he couldn't just walk away. He had to say something to them. If that meant he was going to get a garbage shower, so be it.

Later, he couldn't have said where the words came from. He hadn't prepared anything. But somehow he was able to open his heart and his soul and engage his mind, and it flowed out of him: all the hopes and dreams he had for this country, how he wanted the people to have a voice in their destiny, how he expected to use their input—in short, how he would rule.

He stopped and there was silence. Had he connected at all? He couldn't tell. But at least no one had thrown anything rotten. Not yet.

Then, suddenly, from far back in the crowd came a young, wavering voice. "All hail King Sebastian," it cried.

There was a tittering from the crowd, more embarrassed than amused. But another voice took up the call.

"All hail King Sebastian," it said. And a third voice chimed in, this time one he recognized, Tina Marie.

One by one, others joined the chorus. The sound of it grew and surged. Staring out at them, he couldn't believe it. Maybe they weren't going to hate him after all. Turning, he searched for Emma's face, and when he found it he gestured for her to join him.

She came to his side quickly and he pulled her close. "Your future queen," he called out, and a cheer went up.

"Well, kiss her, then," someone yelled. The crowd laughed, and so did the two of them.

"I'll never pass up a suggestion like that," he said. Turning, he looked down into her radiant face. "I've got to kiss you," he said. "My people demand it."

She laughed through her tears and looked up at him with a love for the ages—and then they came together for a kiss that would make Meridian history.

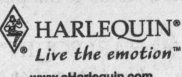

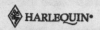
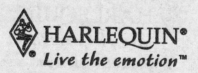

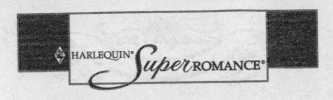

...there's more to the story!

Superromance.
A *big* satisfying read about unforgettable
characters. Each month we offer *six* very different
stories that range from family drama to adventure
and mystery, from highly emotional stories to
romantic comedies—and much more! Stories
about people you'll believe in and care about.
Stories too compelling to put down....

Our authors are among today's *best* romance
writers. You'll find familiar names and talented
newcomers. Many of them are award winners—
and you'll see why!

If you want the biggest and best
in romance fiction, you'll get it
from Superromance!

Emotional, Exciting, Unexpected...

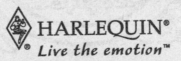

Harlequin Historicals®
Historical Romantic Adventure!

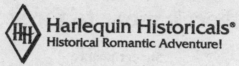

From rugged lawmen and valiant knights to defiant heiresses and spirited frontierswomen, Harlequin Historicals will capture your imagination with their dramatic scope, passion and adventure.

Harlequin Historicals . . . they're too good to miss!

HHDIR104

HARLEQUIN®
INTRIGUE®
WE'LL LEAVE YOU BREATHLESS!

If you've been looking for thrilling tales of
contemporary passion and sensuous love stories
with taut, edge-of-the-seat suspense—then
you'll love Harlequin Intrigue!

Every month, you'll meet six new heroes
who are guaranteed to make your spine tingle
and your pulse pound. With them you'll enter
into the exciting world of Harlequin Intrigue—
where your life is on the line
and so is your heart!

THAT'S INTRIGUE—
ROMANTIC SUSPENSE
AT ITS BEST!

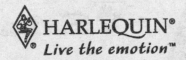

HARLEQUIN®
Live the emotion™

SILHOUETTE *Romance*®

Escape to a place where a kiss is still a kiss...

Feel the breathless connection...

*Fall in love as though it were
the very first time...*

Experience the power of love!

Come to where favorite authors—such as

Diana Palmer, Stella Bagwell, Marie Ferrarella

**and many more—deliver modern fairy tale
romances and genuine emotion,
time after time after time....**

*Silhouette Romance—
from today to forever.*

Silhouette®
Live the possibilities